FOLKTALES OF THE AMUR

FOLKTALES

Stories

OF THE AMUR

from the Russian Far East

by Dmitri Nagishkin

Illustrated by Gennady Pavlishin

Translated by Emily Lehrman

Harry N. Abrams, Inc., Publishers, New York

Contents

Editor: Darlene Geis

Designer: Leslie Stevenson Fry

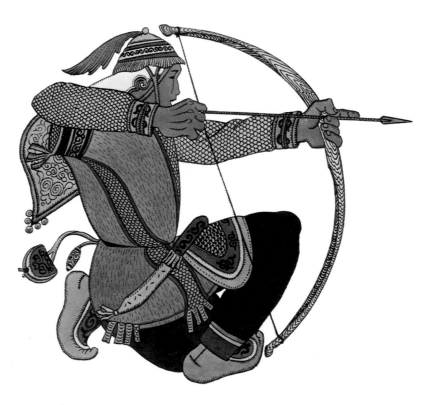

Library of Congress Cataloging in Publication Data

Nagishkin, Dmitri.

      Folktales of the Amur: Stories from the Russian far east.

      SUMMARY: A collection of 31 traditional folktales

from that far eastern part of Russia that lies along

the banks of the Amur River.

  1. Tales, Russian. [1. Folklore—Russia]

I. Pavlishin, Gennady. II. Title.

PZ8.1.N143Fo   398.2'1'0947   79–24067

ISBN 0-8109-0913-8

Library of Congress Catalog Card Number: 79–24067

© 1975 Khabarovsk Publishing House

© 1980 Harry N. Abrams, Inc.

Published in 1980 by Harry N. Abrams, Incorporated, New York

Printed and bound in Japan

The Folktale World
of the Peoples of the Amur

     In this book there are thirty-one short stories, all of them linked by a two-stranded thread that runs through the variegated images and subjects.

     First, there is the connecting strand of nature, with all its amazing contrasts. When we come to the Far East region of the Amur, we see before us a blue Siberian spruce, exactly like the spruce at the Kremlin wall in Red Square in Moscow, but here it is entwined by a subtropical liana, while in its shade are the transparent coral berries of the schisandra. In the fragrant greenery of the Ussuri taiga there is the flutter of dark-blue wings—not the wings of a bird, but of a huge butterfly, the swallowtail.

     Sometimes when we drive through the Amur region, the road in front of our automobile is crossed by an Amur grass snake—a handsome creature, one of the most remarkable reptiles of preglacial times. And there are still tigers among the wild gorges of the Sikhote Alin Mountains. The Amur tiger is a relic—like the ginseng, like the wild grapes of our northern jungles. This tiger is not at all mean and bloodthirsty; he is, rather, a gentleman in the world of predators.

     In the forests along the Amur River live precious sables and snow-white ermine, fiery red foxes, and tree-climbing Himalayan bears. Amur hunters in pursuit of "soft gold" (furs) successfully hunt the huge elk, the fleet-footed

Manchurian deer, and the terrifying wild boar. From time immemorial they have made clothing and ornaments from the fur, have eaten the meat and fat of the beasts and birds.

Every Amur hunter also becomes a fisherman, for in the whole of the Soviet Union it is hard to find a river richer in fish than the Amur. The biggest freshwater fish in the world—the kaluga—lives in its waters. Numerous schools of Siberian salmon run every autumn.

And finally, there are the mountains—blue from a distance, dark green in summer, flaming with all colors in autumn. There are the limitless expanses of the Amur River and the wild, regal beauty of the seashores on which the waves of the Pacific Ocean break. All this is one huge region, our marvelous Far East.

But even this background of natural splendor cannot dim the brightness of that other miracle, man—the second strand in the thread. The Amur peoples' culture was created by man's struggle with nature for thousands of years; their creative imagination found its expression in discoveries beginning with the stone ax, the arrow, and even more clearly, more graphically, in images—in art. One of the greatest riddles in the history of world culture is the existence of this vigorous and expressive art in such small and at first glance (but only at first glance) "primitive" tribes as the Nivkhs or the Nanai. The question of the origin of this richly imaginative and at the same time severe ornamentation of the Amur tribes has excited and continues to excite many generations of scholars.

Excavating in the heavy layers of earth along the Amur, to the depth where Stone Age dwellings occur, we have found many pottery fragments, each an example of the high art of ornamentation. With great excitement we have discovered on them the same characteristic motifs seen on the birchbark utensils made by the Amur people of our century. On these Stone Age vessels are both the spiral and meander, as well executed as similar motifs on the black-glazed vases of ancient Greece. In Kondon and on the wonderful Shchuchy Island, near Mariinsk, sculptures of fired clay have been found lying alongside pottery bowls. These sculptures represent bears, and birds with wings spread wide in flight. There are, as well, portrait sculptures of Stone Age women whose slanting eyes are just like those of the women in our Nanai and Ulch villages.

In a word, the whole artistic world of the Amur peoples' ancestors has opened up before our astonished eyes; and this world, marked by distinctiveness and originality, was at least two thousand years older than ancient Greece and Rome.

This multicolored picture would have been complete if we could have had—related in a living, human voice—the thoughts and events that inspired these artists, whose lips were silenced five thousand years ago. And this miracle happened when we came in contact with the oral folk creation of our day.

Read these tales by Dmitri Nagishkin based upon folk themes of the Udege, Nivkhs, Nanai, Ulches, and others. They embody the life experience of thousands of years, which, together with the mighty power of imagination, carried these forest people forward, raised them above the everyday world, and affirmed the ever-growing power of man over nature. Here were born the first attempts to rise above the earth and to see the people beyond the clouds, who kindle the lights of the evening sky. Here was also born the first attempt to go beyond the bounds of the earth into the cosmos, to look at one's earthly world from the outside and from above.

One hero of the mythical tales, a primordial "cosmonaut," catches the sky as he would a fish—with a wooden hook—and pulls it to earth. He and his brother climb above the clouds to hunt sable, walking and walking around the sky. And this is how the Milky Way, the Road of Heavenly People, was formed along the firmament. Of course, primordial fliers also appear in the tales. They fly on miraculous spears over nine mountains, nine rivers, and nine lakes, over seas and over whole countries. The heroes of these tales rise to heights unattainable by man, to where the Master of Mountains lives. They also descend to the Master of the Sea, even into his yurt.

But the authors of these tales are even more excited by the earth than by the distant sky or by the underwater kingdom. And on earth, they are especially excited by the world of beasts. The central theme of all the stories, their basic subject, is the interrelationship of people and beasts. And could it be otherwise for the inhabitants of the taiga—hunters and fishermen? And so a whole series of stories of taiga people unfolds before us. They are amazing to us who are products of contemporary civilization. These taiga people are bears and, at the same time, they are men "in other shirts," as Dersu Uzala used to say. A bear can turn into a man, a man can fall in love with a she-bear and himself turn into a bear, become a taiga person. For bears and men are brothers; they are related to each other like two different but related clans.

In these tales not only beasts but also plants—birches, for instance— live, reason, and act to help or to harm man. At times they can speak a human language and can even give birth to a human being. Stones too live and reason; stones or birch logs can turn into men, and men can turn to stone.

And it is not at all surprising that in these tales there are so many subjects common to the tales of world folklore. They were born of the earliest clan society of primitive hunters. The similarity of subjects in ancient tales is striking. A lone infant, the hero-fugitive Azmun, sails from no one knows where to the land of the Nivkhs. Similarly the Biblical infant Moses, whom the pharaoh's daughter found in the bulrushes of the Nile, was a hero set adrift on a mighty river. And in Homer, the wanderer Ulysses, cast by the sea onto the shores of Ithaca, recapitulates the theme of the hero as fugitive, the exile.

We know the reason for this similarity of the heroes' fate in myths: long ago, tales were told about culture heroes, ancestors, and forefathers, rather than about kings or czars. The clan elders, its first historians, answering young people's questions—where did our first ancestor come from—would reply, "He sailed down from the headwaters of the river."

Of course, the folktale world of Far Eastern tribes is only a brook flowing into the sea of world folklore. This brook is small but crystal-pure and fresh, filled with reflections of their distinctive life. And it would be a great mistake to try to reduce the contents of these folktales to common stereotypes. Each ethnic group has put into these standard tales its own specific content, has generated its own variegated, kaleidoscopic picture, its own local coloring.

Folktale, myth, legend—all the power of the artistic word and imagination—are used not only to entertain man and fill his heart with gladness. They also serve an educational, moral, and aesthetic purpose for the society that created them.

The Far Eastern scholar and writer, Dmitri Nagishkin, collected the tales of the Amur in their four or five original languages, and then rendered them into clear, straightforward Russian. He had a perfect understanding of the oral traditions of the Far Eastern peoples and, making use of their subjects and language, he created an original artistic work that has been well received among readers not only in the Soviet Union but also abroad.

In his tales, almost as in Shakespeare or Schiller, good and evil contrast and oppose each other in living, concrete images. The evil are those who break the eternal laws of the taiga: share your food with one who is hungry; give help to one who is weak; offer shelter at your hearth to the orphan. Respect the taiga man—the bear; show him the honors established by custom. And don't pour water on the campfire or poke a knife into it—it is alive! It is the protector of you and your fathers, grandfathers, and great-grandfathers!

The community of a primitive society is as tense as a drawn bowstring in its struggle for survival. And for this reason there is no room in it for lazy men and women. Their punishment is inevitable. Expelled from the clan, they turn into birds. The capricious and discontented Lado with her cruel heart becomes a swan; Ayoga, vain and lazy, turns into a goose. Not only are people and beasts ashamed of a trait as disgraceful as laziness, but "things" are also: the knife, the fishing spear, the flint—who become the helpers of the poor man Monokto.

Nor is there room in clan society for cowards, those who have "the heart of a hare." Woe betide the hunter who discovers that the heart in his breast is soft and cowardly. Only after going through the seven fears, the seven trials of manhood, does Indiga find his manly heart.

Braggarts and those who believe them are punished too, mainly in the story of the hares who became walleyed as the penalty for trusting a boaster.

But the traits condemned most strongly are egotism and greed. Thus, the storytellers say about a greedy, rich man: he has a light hand when he takes, but a heavy one when he gives. And a proverb defines greed even more graphically: "A pot without a bottom—whatever you throw into it, it's still empty."

This is the many-colored canvas of our tales—many-colored also because the tales constitute a kind of overall ethnographic encyclopedia as well as a Book of Genesis of the ancient culture of the indigenous peoples of the Far East.

The foregoing pertains not only to the text but, at least equally, to the illustrations, the wonderful pictures produced by the artist and ethnographer Gennady Pavlishin. When one studies this sparkling world of colors and lines, they literally enchant us, bewitch us with their creative power; they captivate us with their romantic incandescence and, at the same time, with their remarkable concreteness, with their accurate rendering of characteristic traits of the life and culture of these peoples.

Surprisingly, traditions of Amur folk art, which are thousands of years old, have thus been regenerated in a new form in the work of a contemporary Russian artist—not as an imitation, but as an original creation.

Thus this remarkable book was born, uniting in a new way the magic of a storyteller's words with the talented brush of an artist.

A. P. Okladnikov
Head of the Siberian Branch
of the USSR Academy of Sciences

The Brave Azmun

To the bold, misfortune never bars the way. The bold will go through fire and flood and only become stronger. People long remember the bold and the brave. Fathers tell tales of the bold and the brave to their sons.

This story took place long ago. Then the Nivkhs still made their arrowheads of stone. Then the Nivkhs still fished with wooden hooks. Then the Amur estuary was called the Little Sea.

In those days there was a village on the very edge of the Amur River.

13

The Nivkhs lived there neither too well nor too badly. When the fish ran heavily, the Nivkhs were merry, sang their songs, ate their fill. When the fish ran lightly, the Nivkhs were quiet, smoked moss in their pipes, and pulled their belts in tighter. One spring this is what happened.

One day some of the men and older boys were sitting on the riverbank, watching the water, smoking their pipes, and mending their nets. They were staring—something was floating down the Amur: five, six, maybe ten trees. A storm must have felled some trees somewhere, and the floodwaters had jammed them together so firmly that you couldn't pull them apart. Soil had fallen on the trees, and grass had grown on them. A whole island was floating by! The Nivkhs saw a whittled pole standing on the island. On that pole two rows of curled wood shavings were stirring and whirring in the wind. A red cloth tied to the pole was flapping in the breeze.

An old Nivkh, Pletun, said, "There's someone on that island. A whittled pole was put there as protection from the evil eye. It means someone is asking for help."

The Nivkhs heard a child's cry coming from the island. A child was crying at the top of his voice.

Pletun said, "There is a child on the island. He must be alone in the world. Evil people killed all his kinfolk, or the Black Death took them all away. A mother wouldn't leave a child without a reason. She must have put him on the island—sent him out to search for good people."

The island came closer. The child's cry sounded louder and louder.

"How can a Nivkh not help!" said Pletun.

The boys threw out a rope with a wooden hook, caught the island, pulled it into shore. They saw a child lying there—all white, round, his black eyes shining like little stars, his face round like a full moon. In his hands the child held an arrow and an oar.

Pletun looked and thought, this child will become a bogatyr—a folk hero. Even in the cradle he holds an arrow and an oar. He is afraid neither of enemy nor of work.

He said, "I will call him my son. I will give him a new name. Let him be called Azmun."

The Nivkhs lifted Azmun in their arms and carried him to Pletun's house. But what was this? With each step the child became heavier and heavier.

They said to the old man, "Hey, Pletun, your son is growing in our arms. Look!"

"How can a man not grow in his own land, in the arms of his own people!" answered Pletun. "A man gets strength from his native land!"

Pletun must have been right, saying that a man's native land gives him strength: by the time they came to the old man's house, Azmun had grown up. The boys carried him as far as the threshold, and at the threshold they set him down on the ground, and he stood on his own feet. He stepped aside, giving way to his elders, and entered the house only after they did.

"Aha!" thought Pletun, looking at his new son. "The boy will do many good deeds for his people—first he thinks of others, then of himself."

And Azmun sat his adopted father on the bunk, bowed to him, and said, "Sit a while, father. You're tired after your long life. Rest a little."

He took the net and the oar. He went out to the boat on the riverbank. The boat leaped into the water, by itself. Azmun stood up in the boat, put down his oar, and the oar began to move by itself, to row the boat to the middle of the river. Then the boat glided off. Azmun cast the net out into the water. He pulled the net in—it was filled with fish. He went home and gave the fish to the women. Everyone in the village ate fish that day.

Time passed, and Azmun said to his adopted father, "There is very little fish here, father."

Pletun answered him, "The fish haven't come. The Amur isn't giving us fish."

"We must ask for fish, father. How can Nivkhs live without fish?"

Before, they had always asked for fish—they had fed the Amur so that it would give them fish.

And so they went to feed the Amur.

They went out in many boats. They wore their best clothes, made of many-colored sealskins. They wore coats of black dog fur. As they sailed, they sang brave songs. When they came to the middle of the Amur, Pletun took some cereal, dried fish, and elk meat. He threw it all into the river.

"We simple people ask you—send us fish, send lots of good fish, different kinds of fish. We are throwing you our dogs' dried fish—we have nothing else to eat. We are starving! Our bellies are stuck to our backs. Help us, and we won't forget you!"

Azmun threw his net into the water, and he pulled in a crowd of fish. The Nivkhs were glad, but Azmun was frowning. "Once—that may just be luck," he said. He cast his net a second time—he pulled in fewer fish. Azmun frowned. He threw his net in a third time—he pulled in the very last fish. After that, whoever threw his net in caught nothing. Even smelts weren't swimming into the net. The fourth time Azmun cast his net he pulled it out empty.

The Nivkhs became dejected. They lighted their pipes. "We will die now!" they said.

Azmun ordered that all the fish be put into one storehouse and everyone be given only a little at a time.

Pletun began to cry and said to Azmun, "I called you my son, I thought I would give you a new life. There is no fish—what will we eat? We will all die of hunger. Go away, my son! Yours is a different road. Go away from us—leave our misfortune on our own doorstep."

Azmun began to think. He lighted his father's pipe. He puffed enough smoke to fill three storehouses. He thought a long time. Then he said, "I will go to Tayrnadz—the Old Man of the Sea. The reason there are no fish in the Amur is that the Master has forgotten all about the Nivkhs."

Pletun became frightened. No Nivkh had ever gone to the Master of the Sea. That had never happened before. How could a mere person go down to the sea bottom to Tayrnadz?

"Are you strong enough for this journey?" asked the father.

Azmun stamped his foot on the earth—he sank into the earth up to his waist from the force of his stamping. He struck a rock with his fist—the rock cracked; out of that crack a spring began to flow. He squinted his eyes and peered at a far-off mound and said, "A squirrel is sitting at the foot of the mound, holding a nut in her teeth; the nut is too hard for her to crack. I will help her!" Azmun took his bow, put in an arrow, pulled on the bowstring, and shot. The arrow flew, hit the nut that the squirrel was holding in her teeth, cracked it in half, and didn't even touch the squirrel.

"I am strong enough!" said Azmun.

Azmun got ready for the journey. He put a little bag of Amur earth in his bosom, took a knife, a bow and some arrows, a rope with a hook at the end, and a bone musical instrument—a *kungakhkei*—to play, in case he felt lonely on the way.

He promised his father that he would send a message about himself soon. He instructed that the fish he had caught be given to everyone to eat until he came back.

And so he went off.

He walked to the seashore. He came to the Little Sea. He saw a seal staring at him from the water, dying of hunger.

Azmun shouted to her, "Hey, neighbor, is it far to the Master?"

"What master do you want?"

"Tayrnadz, the Old Man of the Sea!"

"If he is of the sea, look for him in the sea," the seal answered.

Azmun walked on. He came to the sea of Okhotsk—they called it the Big Sea then. The sea stretched before him—you could not see the end of it. Seagulls were flying over it, cormorants were crying. Waves were rolling, one after the other. A gray sky covered with clouds hung over the sea. Where to look for the Master here? How to get to him? There wasn't even anyone to ask. Azmun looked all around. What to do? He yelled to the seagulls, "Hey, neighbors, is the catch good? There are people dying of hunger!"

"What catch?" the gulls answered. "You can see for yourself, we can barely flap our wings. We haven't seen a fish in a long time. Soon there will be an end to our kind. It looks as though the Old Man of the Sea has fallen asleep, forgotten all about his business."

Azmun said, "I am going to him, neighbors. But I don't know how to get to him."

The seagulls said, "There is an island far out in the sea. Smoke comes out of the island. It's not an island at all but the roof of Tayrnadz's yurt; the smoke comes out of the chimney. We've never seen it, our fathers have never been in it—the migrating birds told us about it. How to get there we don't know. Ask the whales."

"All right," said Azmun.

Azmun walked along the seashore. He walked for a long time, until he grew tired. He sat on the sand among the stones, leaned his head on his arms, and started to think. He thought, and he thought, and he fell asleep. Suddenly, in his sleep, he heard people making a lot of noise on the shore. Azmun half opened his eyes.

He saw several young men playing on the shore: they were chasing one another, playing tug-of-war, playing leapfrog, playing with curved swords. Then some seals came up on shore. The men began to strike the seals with their swords. One blow, and the seal would fall dead on its side. "Oh," thought Azmun, "if only I had a sword like that!" Azmun looked—he saw some worn boats lying on the sand.

Then the men began to wrestle. They threw their swords down, and when they began to fight among themselves, they stopped noticing what went on about them; they yelled, they quarreled. Azmun managed to throw out his rope with the hook, caught one of the swords, and pulled it slowly toward him. He touched the blade with his finger—a good sword! It would come in handy.

The men stopped wrestling. They all took up their swords—all but one of the men, who was missing his. He cried, "Oy-ya-kha! The Master will give it to me now! What will I say to the Old Man? How will I get back to him?"

"Oh-ho," thought Azmun, "they know the Old Man. They must be from the Sea Village!"

And he lay there quietly, not stirring.

The men began to look for the sword—no sword to be found. The one who had lost his sword ran off into the woods to see if maybe he had dropped it there.

The rest pushed the boats off into the sea and got into them. Only one boat remained on shore.

Azmun started after the men. He pushed the empty boat off into the sea and watched where the men were going. He saw that they were rowing out to the open sea. Azmun jumped into the empty boat and also rowed out to sea. Suddenly he looked—what was happening? There were no boats or men ahead! Only whales were swimming in the sea, cutting through the waves; they raised their back fins up like swords, and pieces of seal meat were impaled on the fins. Now Azmun's boat came to life and began to move strangely. Azmun took a good look—he was sitting not in a boat but on a whale's back. Then he understood that it was not boats but whale skins that had been lying on the shore. That it was not men but whales who had been playing with the swords on the shore. And they were not even swords, but the back fins of the whales. "Well, all right," thought Azmun, "at least I'm that much closer to the Old Man."

Whether he sailed this way for a long time I don't know—he didn't say. But he did sail long enough to grow a mustache.

At last Azmun saw an island ahead; it looked like the roof of a yurt. On the highest point of the island was a hole, and from the hole smoke was curling up. "The Old Man must live there!" Azmun said to himself. So Azmun put an arrow to his bow and sent the arrow back to his father.

The whales swam up to the island, threw themselves on the shore, rolled over, and became men—men holding seal meat in their hands.

But the whale under Azmun turned back to sea. There must have been no way for him to get home without his sword! Azmun was toppled into the water, and he almost drowned.

The men saw Azmun thrashing in the sea and came rushing over to him. Azmun scrambled out of the water onto the shore. The men looked him over, frowned, and said, "Who are you? How did you get here?"

"What's the matter with you—don't you recognize one of your own?" said Azmun. "I fell behind while I was looking for my sword. Here it is, my sword!"

"Yes, that is your sword. But why don't you look like yourself?"

Azmun said, "I changed, from fear that I had lost my sword. I still can't get back to myself. I'll go to the Old Man—let him make me look as I did before."

"The Old Man is asleep," the men said. "You see, there is hardly any smoke."

The men went into their own yurts. They left Azmun standing alone.

Azmun began to climb the hill. He climbed halfway and came to a village. There were only girls in that village. They barred Azmun's way and wouldn't let him go any farther.

"The Old Man is asleep; he said not to disturb him!" They crowded around him, making up to him. "Don't go to Tayrnadz! Stay with us! You'll take a wife—you'll live well!"

And the girls were beauties—one more beautiful than the other. Clear eyes, lovely faces, lithe bodies, deft hands. Such beautiful girls that Azmun thought it wouldn't be a bad idea for him to take a wife from among them.

Then the Amur earth in its little bag stirred in Azmun's bosom. Azmun remembered that he hadn't come here to take a bride, but he couldn't break loose from the girls. A bright thought struck him: he took some beads out of his tunic and threw them on the ground.

The girls flung themselves down to pick up the beads, and Azmun saw that instead of feet they had flippers. They were not girls at all, but seals!

While the seal girls were busy gathering the beads, Azmun went on to the highest point of the hill. He threw his rope through the hole at the top. He attached the hook to the rim of the hole and climbed down the rope. When he got to the bottom, he found himself in the home of the Old Man of the Sea.

He dropped to the floor, hurting himself a little. He looked around.

Everything in the house was like a Nivkh's house: a bunk, a hearth, walls, posts—only here everything was covered with fish scales. And outside the window was water instead of sky.

Outside the window water was splashing, green waves were rolling, seaweed was swaying in the waves like some fantastic forest. Past the windows swam fish, but such fish as no Nivkh would take in his mouth: toothy and bony, and looking to see—whom to swallow!

The Old Man was lying on the bunk, asleep. His gray hair was spread across the pillow. A pipe sticking out of his mouth was scarcely lit, the smoke barely coming out of it, drifting up the chimney. Tayrnadz snored away, hearing nothing. Azmun touched him with his hand—no, the Old Man wouldn't wake up, and that's all there was to it.

Azmun remembered his musical instrument, the *kungakhkei*. He took it out of his bosom, gripped it between his teeth, and plucked at its tongue. The *kungakhkei* began to vibrate, to hum, to buzz—now chirping like a bird, now babbling like a brook, now buzzing like a bee.

Tayrnadz had never heard anything like it. What was it? He stirred, he awoke, he rubbed his eyes, he sat up, putting his legs under him. He was big, like a reef; his face was kind, and his mustache hung down like a catfish's. The scales on his skin were iridescent, like mother-of-pearl. His clothing was made of seaweed. He saw a little fellow standing before him, like a smelt before a sturgeon, holding something in his mouth and playing it so well that Tayrnadz's heart began to jump. Instantly Tayrnadz was awake. He turned his kind face to Azmun, squinted at him, and asked, "Of what people are you?"

"I'm Azmun, of the Nivkh people."

"The Nivkhs live on Sakhalin Island and on the shores of the Little Sea. Why did you travel so far, into our waters and lands?"

Azmun told what misfortune had come to the Nivkhs and bowed to the Old Man.

"Father, help the Nivkhs—send fish to the Nivkhs! Father, the Nivkhs are dying of hunger! They sent me to ask for help."

Tayrnadz became embarrassed. He blushed and said, "A bad thing happened—I lay down only to rest, and I fell asleep! Thank you for waking me!"

Tayrnadz put his hand under his bunk. Azmun looked and saw a huge tank there: in that tank giant kaluga, sturgeon, trout, and all kinds of salmon were swimming. More fish than you've ever seen!

There was a skin lying next to the tank. The Old Man took the skin, filled it a quarter full of fish. He opened the door, threw the fish into the sea, and said, "Swim to the Nivkhs on Sakhalin and on the Amur. Swim fast! Be a good catch in the spring."

"Father," said Azmun, "don't stint on the fish for the Nivkhs."

Tayrnadz frowned.

Azmun got scared. "Well, now I am lost!" he thought. "I made the Old Man angry. It will be bad for me!" Then he thought of his father and stood up tall, looking straight into Tayrnadz's eyes.

Tayrnadz smiled. "I would not have forgiven anyone else for interfering with my business, but I'll forgive you; I see you are not thinking of yourself but of others. Let it be your way."

Tayrnadz threw another half a skin of all kinds of fish into the sea. "Swim to Sakhalin and to the Amur. Be a good catch in the fall."

Azmun bowed to him. "Father! I am poor—I don't have anything to repay you for your kindness. Take my *kungakhkei* as a present."

He gave Tayrnadz his musical instrument, first showing him how to play it.

And the Old Man had long been itching to have it; he couldn't take his eyes off it! He liked the toy so much.

Tayrnadz was happy. He took the *kungakhkei* into his mouth, gripped it between his teeth, plucked at its tongue.

The *kungakhkei* began to hum and to buzz, now like the sea wind, now like the surf, now like the rustle of the trees, now like a bird at dawn, now like a gopher whistling. Tayrnadz was playing and making merry. He started to walk about the house, then to dance. The house began to shake, outside the windows the waves raged, seaweed was being torn to pieces—a storm was rising in the sea.

Azmun saw that Tayrnadz was too busy for him now. He went to the chimney, took hold of his rope, and began to climb up. As he climbed his hands got scratched until they bled; while he'd been visiting the Old Man, the rope had become covered with sharp sea shells.

He climbed out and looked around.

The seal girls were still searching for the beads, quarreling about how to divide them among themselves. They had forgotten all about their houses, and the doors were now overgrown with moss!

Azmun looked at the lower village—it was empty, but far out at sea he could see the whales' fins. The whales were chasing the fish to the shores of the Big Sea, to the shores of the Little Sea, to the Amur!

How was he to get home now?

Azmun saw a rainbow hanging in the sky. One end was resting on the island, the other on the Big Land.

And in the sea, waves were raging—Tayrnadz was dancing in his yurt. White crests were breaking on the sea.

Azmun climbed onto the rainbow. He barely made it. He got all smudged—his face was green, his hands yellow, his belly red, his feet blue. He scrambled up somehow and ran along the rainbow to the Big Land. As he ran his feet kept slipping through; he could scarcely keep from falling. Then he looked down and saw the sea turning black with fish. The Nivkhs will have fish!

He came to the end of the rainbow.

Azmun jumped to earth. On the seashore, sitting near a boat, was the man-whale whose sword Azmun had taken. Azmun recognized him and gave him back his sword. The man grabbed it.

"Thank you," he said, "I thought I'd never see my home again. I won't forget your kindness; I will chase the fish right up to the Amur. I don't hold a grudge against you. I know now that you did it for your people, not for yourself."

Rolling over, he became a whale again. He raised up his sword—his back fin—and swam out to sea.

Azmun walked to the Big Sea; he came to the shore. He met seagulls and cormorants. They yelled to him, "Hey, neighbor! Did you visit the Old Man?"

"Yes," Azmun yelled back to them. "Don't look at me, look at the sea!"

And the fish were running in the sea, the water was foaming. The gulls flung themselves at the fish, growing fat before his very eyes.

And Azmun walked farther. He passed the Little Sea; he was coming to the Amur. He saw the seal who was almost dead. The seal asked him, "Did you visit the Old Man?"

"Yes," said Azmun. "Don't look at me, look at the Little Sea!"

And the fish were running in the estuary, the water was foaming. The seal threw herself at the fish. She began to eat the fish, growing fat before his very eyes.

And Azmun walked farther. He came to his own village. The Nivkhs were sitting on the bank, barely alive; they had smoked up all the moss, they had eaten all the fish.

Pletun came out to the threshold of his house to meet his son and kissed him on both cheeks.

"Did you visit the Old Man, my son?" he asked.

"Father, don't look at me, look at the Amur!" answered Azmun.

And on the Amur the water was seething—so many fish had come. Azmun threw his spear into the shoal. The spear stood up on end and moved along with the fish. Azmun said, "Will there be enough fish, my adopted father?"

"There will be enough."

The Nivkhs began to live well. Fish were running in the spring and in the fall! Since that time the Nivkhs have forgotten many people. But to this day they remember Azmun and his *kungakhkei*.

When the sea becomes stormy, waves surge onto the rocky shore, white crests break on the waves—and in the whistle of the sea wind you can hear now the cry of a bird, now the whistle of a gopher, or now the rustle of the trees. That's the Old Man of the Sea; in order not to fall asleep, he is playing on the *kungakhkei* and dancing in his yurt under the sea.

How the Bear and the Chipmunk Stopped Being Friends

When the Khingan Mountains were still small, when you could still shoot an arrow and hear it fall on the other side of the Khingan, that's when the bear and the chipmunk were friends.

A bear and a chipmunk lived together in one lair. They hunted together. They shared everything equally. What the bear would get, the chipmunk would eat; what the chipmunk would get, the bear would eat. They were friends like this for a long time. But as everybody knows, to the envious such a friendship is like a speck in the eye. They won't rest until they've put an end to it.

One day the chipmunk came out of his lair; he felt like cracking some nuts. He met a fox who waved her red tail, greeted him, and asked, "How are you doing, neighbor?"

The chipmunk told her all about his life with the bear.

The fox listened to what the chipmunk said, and it made her envious: two animals lived together without quarreling. She herself was friends with no one, because she was crafty and always on the lookout to cheat.

She pretended to feel sorry for the chipmunk. She folded her paws on her belly and shed a tear—everybody knows how easy it is for a cheat to start crying. She said, "You poor thing! I feel so sorry for you."

The chipmunk became anxious. "Why do you feel sorry for me, neighbor?"

"Silly!" answered the fox. "The bear takes advantage of you, and you don't even realize it."

"What do you mean, takes advantage?" asked the chipmunk.

"This is what I mean. When the bear kills an animal, who is the first to tear it with his teeth?"

"Brother bear," answered the chipmunk.

"See, that's how he gets the best piece. You probably haven't seen a good piece of meat in a long time; all you get to eat is the bear's leftovers! That's why you've never grown big."

The fox flirted her tail, wiped her tears, and shook her head.

"Well, good-bye," she said finally. "I see you like this kind of life. But if I were you, I would be the first to get my teeth into the meat!"

And the fox ran off, as though she had business somewhere else, covering her tracks with her tail.

The chipmunk looked after her and thought, "Maybe the fox figured things out right." He thought so hard he forgot all about the nuts he was going to crack. "Well," he said to himself, "what a cheat the bear has turned out to be. And I trusted him; I even looked up to him as an older brother."

A little later the bear and the chipmunk went hunting.

On the way they walked through a raspberry patch. The bear grabbed a raspberry stem in his paws, started to eat the berries, and invited his brother

to do the same. The chipmunk watched. The fox was right! The bear was the first to taste the berries.

The bear caught a gopher and called to the chipmunk. The chipmunk watched. The bear was the first to sink his claws into the gopher. The fox was right!

The brothers came on a beehive inside a small oak tree. The bear pushed the oak branch aside, held it out of the way with his paw, and thrust his snout into the hive. He was puffing out his nostrils, smacking his lips. He called his brother to come taste the honey. And the chipmunk watched. The bear was again the first to take a taste. The fox was right again!

The chipmunk became angry. "Well," he thought, "I'll teach you!"

They went hunting another time.

The chipmunk sat on the back of his brother's neck—he couldn't possibly keep up with the bear on his small legs.

The bear sniffed out game. He caught a wild goat. As he was about to grab it with his teeth, the chipmunk jumped up between the bear's ears! He did it so he could sink his teeth into the goat ahead of his brother, take the best piece for himself, and so get a little bigger. The bear was startled, let go of the goat, and off it ran.

Both brothers were left hungry.

They went on.

The bear saw a gopher, crept up to it, but again the chipmunk jumped between his ears! Again the bear was startled half to death. Again the animal got away. The bear grew angry but said nothing to his brother.

They met a young boar. At any other time the bear would not have started up with a boar, but now hunger made his belly stick to his ribs. He was so angry he went after the boar! He roared so loudly that the boar was frightened and began to back away from the bear. He kept backing away until his tail bumped into a tree—he could move no farther. Then the bear pressed after him. He opened his jaws, snapping his teeth as though he would swallow the boar whole!

No sooner did he reach the animal than the chipmunk jumped from between his ears onto the boar! He wanted to be the first to have a taste. The bear became furious. To keep the chipmunk from getting underfoot, he struck him so hard with his paw that all five claws sank into the chipmunk's back.

The chipmunk tore himself away—ripping his hide from head to tail.

Howling with pain, he jumped into a tree, then into another, and then into still another. He kept jumping from branch to branch until he was out of the bear's sight.

The bear finished killing the boar and called to his brother. "Hey, brother! Come eat the fresh meat!"

But there was no chipmunk; it was as though there had never been one.

The bear went home. He waited and waited for his brother, but he never came.

The chipmunk ran away. He lived in trees for a long time, until the wounds on his back healed. Well, the wounds healed all right, but five black stripes from the bear's claws remained for the rest of his life.

Now the chipmunk won't go near the bear and won't eat meat any more. And if he finds himself near a bear, he angrily throws cedar cones at the bear. And whenever the bear raises his head, the chipmunk runs away—completely out of sight!

A Great Misfortune

Old men have their lives behind them. Old men know a great deal—they can always give good advice. But a young man has words of wisdom, too: his body is stronger, his eyes are better, his hands are steadier; his whole life lies before him, so he looks ahead.

A long time ago the Udege lived where it was warm—in the valley, along the seashore. There were so many of them they were like trees in a forest. They lived quietly, didn't fight with anybody. They hunted animals, caught fish, obeyed the law, raised their children. That was a long time ago.

In one village the old shaman Kandiga was chief in those days. When anybody got sick, Kandiga would take out his tambour with its picture of Agdy—Thunder. He would light a fire, warm the tambour over the flames, and begin to make magic. He stepped around the fire, dancing; he spoke all kinds of words, singing; he beat on his tambour with a carved stick, and it roared like thunder. Kandiga said that when he beat on his tambour he frightened the evil demons away. He raised such a racket that echoes answered for the next two days. Sometimes the sick person did get well. But if he died, the shaman did his job then too. He took the dead man's soul to Buni, the underworld kingdom, on the back of a gray bird with a red beak. It is true that no one had ever seen the gray bird; but how could you not trust the shaman?

All the people in the clan feared the shaman, and they all obeyed him. Whatever the shaman wanted to take, they gave him. Whatever the shaman told them to do, they did. How could you not give the shaman what he wanted? If you didn't, he would let evil demons loose upon the village, and it would be bad for everybody. They said Kandiga was a very great shaman. The demons loved him. Kandiga had plenty of everything, even when all the other Udege went hungry and had to chew their goatskin boots for food.

In the village lived a young man, Dimdiga. He was a good hunter: he could kill two geese with one arrow. A young man he was, no worse than the others, but, in fact, even better than most. This young man would often wonder about Kandiga, and he could make no sense of one thing: why was it that events happened this way? If he killed two ducks, he could take only one for himself and had to give the other to Kandiga; if he killed two sables, one would be for himself, the other again for Kandiga. Kandiga didn't go hunting, he didn't get wet in the swamp, he didn't get parched in the sun, he didn't freeze in the frost; yet he got as much game as Dimdiga. Why?

At the men's council meeting Kandiga would say, as he divided the game, "We did well, everybody is pleased."

But finally Dimdiga spoke up. "Chief! I am not pleased. Why are things this way? You sit in your yurt, you spare your feet. Every man gives you half of everything he has. Why do I—a hunter—own less than you?"

"See how stupid you are!" Kandiga said. "It is the spirits that bring me luck. Why? Ask them. But watch out! I'll call all my demons now!"

He put on his hat with the antlers and his belt with the rattles, and he grabbed his thundering tambour. The tambour roared—the thunder rolled out over the whole countryside.

The old men begged, "Please don't make magic against us. Don't listen to that young man! He caught only animals when he went hunting; he never caught any brains."

"All right," the shaman said. "I will forgive him, but only for your sake."

So Dimdiga went hunting again. Whenever he killed animals, there was one for himself and another for Kandiga. Still the shaman kept reviling Dimdiga; whatever the young man said seemed wrong to the shaman.

That year people from faraway villages came running to this village. They were ragged and hungry. They were crying. They said, "Terrible people attacked us. They are a great multitude! They are like tigers. They ride on top of wild animals."

"What animals?" Dimdiga asked at the council meeting. "Dogs?"

"No, not dogs."

"Reindeer?"

"No, not reindeer. Don't we know reindeer? We've kept reindeer all our lives. These animals have four legs, smooth skins, faces like reindeer, but not quite; these animals' tails are long, their feet have round hooves, and the hair on their neck is long, too. When these animals yell, you can hear them from afar. The hearts of those who hear these yells become hares' hearts. The terrible people have no mercy on anyone. They kill the men, carry off the women, and throw the children under the hooves of their animals."

"Bad people!" Dimdiga said. "We must leave because we do not have enough strength to fight them."

"They are not people," Kandiga said.

"But we saw them ourselves: they are people, with two arms, two legs, one head. They speak a foreign language. They leave only ashes in the villages. Wherever they pass, even the grass no longer grows."

"They are not people," Kandiga said. "They are evil demons. Dimdiga made them come. There aren't any such people. Bring me your gifts. I will make magic, and I will chase these demons away!"

The people from the faraway villages ran farther.

Then people from nearby villages came running.

"Run!" they cried. "Evil people attacked us. We didn't have enough strength to fight them. They burn the yurts, they kill our people!"

"We must leave," Dimdiga said at the council meeting. "Evil demons don't burn yurts."

"These are not people," Kandiga insisted, "they are evil demons! There is no demon that can frighten me. I will make magic and I will scare away all the demons! Bring me your gifts."

The people from the nearby villages ran farther.

At last people from neighboring villages came running.

"These evil people are called Mungals! Folks say they have roved over the whole world and left nobody alive! The only ones still alive are you and us."

"Do the Mungals get off their animals?" asked Dimdiga at the council meeting.

"They get off when they eat and when they kill."

"What do the Mungals eat?"

"Their surplus animals."

"They are people," Dimdiga said. "We must get our weapons ready; we must get out of their way. What do the Mungals' animals eat?"

"Grass," the people answered.

"We must go into the forests, into the mountains," said Dimdiga. "These people are probably not used to forests and mountains."

"They are demons!" said Kandiga. "They are evil spirits whom Dimdiga made angry. Bring me your gifts. I will drive all these misfortunes away. I will build an idol—Mangni—and I will chase away all the demons!"

Kandiga began to make magic day and night. He would fall down exhausted, but then jump up and start making magic again. He built a terrifying idol—Mangni—and kept circling around and around him.

Mangni stood on a hillock. He was the height of three men.

His stomach was hollow—so he would always be hungry; his arms were entwined by serpents—so he would be supple in battle. On his feet he had lizards—so he would run fast. In his breast he had a bird instead of a heart. On his chest he wore a polished brass plate, shining like the sun, for blinding the enemy. Everything was reflected in that brass plate.

Kandiga said, "The Mungals will come galloping on their animals, they will see themselves in the brass plate, they'll think no one's here but them. They will go away."

"We must drive the Mungals away with spears and arrows," said Dimdiga.

The people huddled up to Kandiga. They believed there was no one else to protect them.

Kandiga built two more idols—to help Mangni beat the demons.

Then Dimdiga said, "Listen, people, great misfortune has come. It is not up to old man Kandiga to drive it away. Take your bows and arrows, your spears; go to the forests and to the mountains! The Mungals' animals need grass. When the Mungals reach the forests and the mountains, they will find nothing to feed their animals; they will turn back!"

An uproar arose in the village.

The young men cried, "Dimdiga is right—men must fight!"

The old men wailed, "Nobody has strength enough to stand up against the demons!"

And the Mungals were already near. The villagers could already hear their yells. They could already see the flames: the Mungals were burning the yurts of Dimdiga's fellow tribesmen.

Kandiga was making magic. Foam was frothing at his lips. His tambour was roaring like thunder. The rattles at his belt were jingling. His antler hat was swaying. Watching him, old men shook with fright.

Dimdiga said to his kinsmen, "Whoever is coming with me, cross the brook! Whoever has pity for his children, cross the brook! Whoever is not ashamed to take up weapons, go across!"

Whoever did not trust the shaman went across the brook. Those who believed more in demons than in themselves remained with the shaman.

Dimdiga left.

And the Mungals came like a storm cloud. There were as many Mungals as grains of sand on the seashore! The earth shook from the clatter of horses' hooves. Over and around the Mungals there was noise like the noise at floodtime: they yelled, they whooped, they urged their animals on. They had long curved swords in their hands, quivers with arrows over their shoulders, battle axes at their saddles. Dimdiga was right: the Mungals were not demons, but people.

When the Mungals saw the village, they began to yell even louder. They shot off such a storm cloud of arrows that you couldn't see the sun!

But Dimdiga and his people were already close to the forest.

The Mungals saw Dimdiga and sped after him. They almost caught up with him. But he had already entered the forest. Dimdiga drove the women and children farther into the forest. And he and the men hid behind the trees.

They started shooting their arrows at the Mungals from their taut bows. The arrows began to sing and fly. An arrow would have passed right

through a demon: how could a man kill a demon? But the Mungals were falling out of their saddles, pierced by arrows.

From tree to tree, deeper into the forest went Dimdiga. From tree to tree, deeper into the forest also went the villagers who had come with him.

The Mungals chased Dimdiga for a long time. But their animals weren't used to the forest. The animals felt cramped in the forest. The Mungals had no place to graze them. There was nothing to feed the animals in the forest. Only gray moss hung from the trees all around, and the ferns stood up like a wall.

The Mungals turned back.

Dimdiga sent his people to tell all his fellow tribesmen how to save themselves from the Mungals. The Udege left their villages. Long lines of the Udege people stretched out from the valley and the seashore to the forests and the mountains. They started living in the mountains and the forests. The Udege became the Forest People. And that's what they are called to this day.

How much time passed, I don't know. Dimdiga went to his old village. He wanted to see if Mangni and the other idols had helped Kandiga.

Dimdiga saw that the Mungals had ridden as far as the sea, then turned back and returned to their steppes.

In his old village Dimdiga saw Mangni lying on the ground, defeated. Grass was growing in his hollow belly; lizards were running around in his hollow breast. His helpers were also lying on the ground, all charred—the Mungals had made a campfire out of them.

Dimdiga saw the shaman lying on the ground, his legs spread out, an ax in his hands. Next to him a Mungal was lying, killed by an ax. The shaman must have thought of Dimdiga, finally, but it was too late. And now Kandiga was lying on the ground, a black raven sitting on his chest. Polecats and wolverines roamed the village.

Dimdiga went back to the forest. He said to his kinsmen, "The forest and the rocks are our best protection!"

From then on the Udege live in the forests. At the council meetings, the young men listen to the old men. But the old men expect a wise word from the young men, too.

38

The Cuckoo's Riches

Never be afraid of work. If you don't bestir yourself, fortune will pass you by and disappear.

Once three brothers lived in a village. They were named Khalba, Adunga, and Pokcho.

The two older brothers, Khalba and Adunga, liked to hunt, and they often went into the taiga. They knew how to set traps for animals. And with an arrow, they could hit a moving squirrel in the eye. But the youngest brother always lagged behind. When the older brothers went hunting sable, Pokcho went too. The older brothers would build a tent, make a campfire, bow to the Master of the Taiga—so that they would have luck—and off they would go into the taiga. But Pokcho would remain in the tent, cooking the cereal, counting the stars in the sky, thinking to himself, "I wish I had a lot of sables!" and waiting for his share of his brothers' catch. But since all he did was just sit there, his share was only one tenth of what was caught. And that is why, of the three brothers, Pokcho was the poorest. His greatest joy was when his brothers would catch a bear; at that feast he would stuff himself. When it came to eating, Pokcho was always the champion!

The older brothers liked to fish, and they often went out on the river. They knew how to build boats. They could weave nets. They could fish with fishhooks. They could kill a kaluga with one blow. They could even catch three fish at one time with a triple fishhook. Pokcho would be there too—sitting on the riverbank, throwing twigs onto the fire, counting the leaves on the trees, thinking to himself, "I wish I had a lot of fish!" and waiting for his share of his brothers' catch. Again his share was only one tenth. You can't get rich on that! His greatest joy was when his brothers would catch a big kaluga; then he would stuff himself. Everybody ate and ate, but nobody could keep up with Pokcho when it came to eating.

And that is how the brothers lived.

Pokcho envied Khalba and Adunga. The more time passed, the richer they became. And the poorer Pokcho.

Pokcho wanted so much to get rich! When he went walking, he looked at the ground—maybe he would find a bear's tooth; they say it brings riches. If Pokcho found a rag on the ground, he put it in his tunic right away; maybe it would turn out to be a lucky rag and bring him riches! He carefully examined the larch trees—where was that lucky larch on which fir cones grow?

One day Pokcho went into the taiga with his brothers.

The older brothers went hunting; Pokcho went into the tent.

He sat there, cooking the cereal. He was thinking, "Oh, if I could get as many sables as there are grains in this cereal, how well I would live!"

Suddenly a dry branch fell down near him. Pokcho raised his head and saw a cuckoo bird sitting in a pine tree; she was preening herself, waving her tail up and down.

"There will be a lot of berries this fall," Pokcho thought aloud. "This is an old sign."

Thinking of signs, he remembered something that made him jump to his feet. The old men said that if you kill a cuckoo, eat it, then fall asleep and sweat in your sleep, riches will come right into your hands by themselves.

Lazy though Pokcho was, he now bestirred himself. Fortune was about to come into his hands by itself—how could he let it slip away? He grabbed the pot and threw the cereal at the cuckoo. Covered all over with the hot, sticky cereal, the bird fell to the ground. Pokcho ate all of it, even the feathers and the innards. Then he lay down on his side, curled himself up, and fell asleep.

Soon he felt very hot.

Pokcho opened his eyes. What a wonder—sables were marching one by one out of the taiga! A big sable, black as coal, was at the head of the procession, his fur shining so brightly that it hurt your eyes to look at it. Lazy Pokcho was stunned—the Master of Sables himself had come out of the taiga! "What a cuckoo bird that was!" Pokcho rejoiced.

The Master of Sables came straight at Pokcho. He came right up to him, jumped into the air, and disappeared. And the sables that were behind the Master marched right into Pokcho's hands. Pokcho didn't lose his head; he grabbed a big spoon and started to kill the sables with it. As soon as he knocked one on the snout, another would stand at the ready. Pokcho finally grew tired; he had piled up a whole mountain of animals on his right. He heard the Master of Sables asking him from above, "Is that enough, Pokcho?"

"More, more!" yelled Pokcho.

He switched hands and started throwing the dead sables to the left. He piled up a mountain so high that you couldn't see the forest behind it.

"Is that enough, Pokcho?" the Master of Sables asked him again.

"More, more!" Pokcho yelled again.

He grabbed the spoon hard with both hands and kept hitting the sables. Now a whole mountain of sables grew in front of him as well.

Pokcho was exhausted. The Master of Sables asked him the third time, "Is that enough, Pokcho? Without taking a step, you have killed more sables than a hundred hunters would get in a whole season."

Pokcho was about to shout, "More, more!" but he was almost suffocating beneath the piles of sables.

"Enough!" he gasped.

The older brothers came back from the taiga. They looked for the tent, but they couldn't see it under the piles of sables; all they could see was Pokcho's boots sticking out from under the furs.

They pulled their brother out and stood him on his feet.

Pokcho sat down. He lit his pipe and said, "I'm tired, I'll sit and rest a while. You skin the sables."

The older brothers started taking off the skins. They worked for a long time, until they were drenched with sweat. The snow melted under them, the earth thawed, the green grass began to grow. Steam hung over them like a cloud, and a rainbow played in it.

And Pokcho kept hurrying his brothers and shouting at them to be quick.

The older brothers finished their work.

Then, out of nowhere, sleds drawn by dog teams started coming toward Pokcho, one by one. Each dog was finer than the next. They were all white with black paws, and they wore elkskin harnesses with brass buttons. The pelts loaded themselves onto the sleds.

The brothers rode to the village.

High on the first sled sat Pokcho, very self-important.

When he and his brothers arrived at the village, the merchants were already waiting for him.

The merchants started to bargain and haggle, fighting with each other over the sables. The pelts were so good! The merchants gave Pokcho two basketsful of silver, more robes than you could count, grain, flour, sweets—enough to fill a whole storehouse!

Pokcho became so rich that all his kinsmen bowed down to him.

And Pokcho's fortune kept falling on his head, like snow.

Pokcho sent his brothers out to check on his fishnets. The brothers went to the river and started to pull the nets in—but they didn't have enough strength, the catch was so rich! They called the whole village out to help. Together the villagers just managed to pull the nets in. And the fish in the nets were not small and worthless—they were all kaluga fish. In that one catch there was enough fish to feed the whole village for a whole year. Wasn't that something!

Pokcho became the most important person in the village.

Now Pokcho was a generous young man. He decided, in his joy, to give the whole village a treat. He cooked up an enormous potful of cereal—he used up all his grain and all his flour. Pokcho called in all the villagers and said, "Eat as much as you want!"

The villagers came and sat around the pot.

The old men said, "First we must feed the children."

"That's right," Pokcho agreed. "Let the children eat first."

A little boy came up to the pot, with a little spoon in his hand.

Pokcho said to him, "Take a big spoon."

The little boy answered, "It's all right—I don't need much."

The boy dipped his little spoon into the cereal and emptied the whole pot all at once.

"It's good, but there isn't enough," he said.

Pokcho stared at the pot. How did this happen?

And the villagers were insulted. "What is this, Pokcho? You promised to feed the whole village, and you couldn't even give one little boy enough cereal. You see, he is licking his lips—he'd eat some more, but there isn't any."

"Never mind," said Pokcho. "I'll buy some more grain. Call the merchant in here."

The villagers ran after the grain merchant.

Pokcho untied the basket that held his money. The coins jumped out of the basket by themselves and rolled down the road along which the merchants had come. Pokcho tried to hold them back, but it was no use. The money poured through his fingers like water. Pokcho looked: both baskets were lying empty.

"Never mind," said Pokcho. "How can I not treat the villagers to a meal? I'll feed them even if I have to sell my robes!"

He went to the storehouse. All kinds of robes were hanging there: quilted robes; silk robes; robes of fishskin, of elkskin, of reindeer fur; robes sewn with silk thread and with reindeer hair; robes with golden dragons woven into them; robes with buttons of brass, silver, and gold. Pokcho started carrying the robes out of the storehouse. He shouted to the villagers to call another merchant.

But the villagers said to him, "What is it that you are going to sell, Pokcho?"

"What do you mean, 'what'?" Pokcho asked.

Then he looked down and saw that he was carrying birch bark, pecked full of holes by a woodpecker.

And the storehouses were full of birch bark.

Pokcho shouted, "Never mind! I ate the cuckoo bird—I am lucky now! Let's eat the kaluga. I caught enough for a whole year!"

"Well," the villagers said to Pokcho, "there isn't any more kaluga!"

"Where is it, then?" asked Pokcho.

"The cuckoo bird pecked it all up."

"How do you mean, 'pecked it all up'?"

"This is how: the cuckoo flew over to the kaluga, perched on its head, pecked at its eye, and the whole kaluga disappeared! You said you ate the cuckoo, but it looks as though it has eaten you."

The villagers left.

Pokcho, heavy with grief, lay down to sleep.

This was something he knew very well how to do! He heard the villagers shouting, "Hey, Pokcho, wake up! Don't sleep! You'll sleep your whole life away!"

Pokcho felt ashamed. He grew very hot, so hot that he woke up.

He looked around and saw that he was in a hunting tent; the campfire was burning so brightly that it was spreading toward him—even his boots had buckled from the heat.

Pokcho lit his pipe. He thought a while. He thought some more. He looked—and saw that right next to the tent there were fresh sable tracks. The sable must have passed by while Pokcho was dreaming.

Lazy Pokcho jumped up. He grabbed his bow. He put on his skis. He followed the sable tracks.

"Ah," he said. "One sable, caught with your own hands, is better than all of the cuckoo-bird's riches!"

And he may have been right, at that.

Choril and Cholchinay

Both love and friendship are hard to find. To achieve a good life, blessed with both, you must go through many hardships. Even to whittle a stick you must work, and for your friend or for your love you must spare neither hands nor head.

At the time when the Nivkhs were still numerous, Choril, a boy from the Takhta clan, and Cholchinay, a girl from the Chilbi clan, lived on Sakhalin Island. When Cholchinay was born, Choril's mother tied a dog's hair around her arm. Thus Cholchinay became Choril's betrothed.

On the very day that the little girl picked up her first doll, Choril hunted down his first sable. When Cholchinay first picked up a knife to clean a fish, Choril first raised his voice as a man and a hunter in the men's council.

Choril made Cholchinay a doll out of wood. And he made her a little knife. He also made her a board for working fishskins, and he carved it more beautifully than anyone had ever done before.

And that is how they lived.

But you cannot go through life without sorrow.

The Black Death came to the island. Whether the merchants brought it from the Nipponese Islands, whether it was brought by kinsmen from the Amur, whether the wind—the Typhoon—brought it on his black wings, or it came by itself over the seas—who knows? Later, when it left, no one saw where it went, either. It had come alone, but it left carrying many Nivkhs away with it. In every home there was someone dead. In every home tears flowed.

The Black Death carried away Cholchinay's parents, and it took Choril's parents too. Both were left orphans.

So Choril took his betrothed into his home, and they lived together.

Choril brought home a catch every day. He was such a good fisherman that no fish could escape him. He was such a good hunter that no animal got away from him. Choril had a steady hand, a sharp eye. He was handsome, spoke in a firm voice, knew how to sing. He could do everything. Whatever Cholchinay touched, Choril had made with his own hands: he had woven a net, had built a boat, and had made a knife, a spear, a staff, a fish spear, an oar, some drinking cups, and bowls of birch bark. Choril had even made a silver mirror for his betrothed.

Cholchinay grew more beautiful every day. Her eyes were bright like the stars; her lips looked as if they were sprayed with raspberry juice; her eyebrows were like two sables arching over her eyes; and her eyelashes were so long that people made up a saying about them: "Rushes grow around a deep lake."

Soon it would be time for Cholchinay to plait her hair into two braids. Soon it would be time for her to marry Choril. Whenever he looked at his bride-to-be, Choril's heart beat like a swallow's wings.

Choril was already preparing for the wedding.

Whenever he returned from the hunt, he brought back such a catch that you couldn't see him under the pelts.

Whenever he returned from fishing, his catch was so big that the whole village had to help carry it.

Cholchinay would look at him and ask, "Why are you so lucky in everything you do, Choril?"

Choril would look at his Cholchinay, throw back his head, and begin to sing so beautifully that Cholchinay's heart would stand still.

"Ann-n-ga! Unn-g-ga!" Choril sang. "Always think of your love! Then will your heart beat and your eyes shine! Then will your feet run faster and your hands work better! Then will you move boulders as though they were pebbles! Then will you fly over mountains and rivers! Then will the sea be like a handful of water to you! Then no one can stop you! Always think of your love! Then will you be stronger than all your enemies!"

One day Cholchinay went walking in the village. She was the most beautiful girl there. Her voice was like a bird's. She wore a coat of black dog fur. Her skirt was made of many-colored sealskin. Her hat was made of squirrel pelts.

Old Allykh of the Udan-Khingan clan saw Choril's bride-to-be. He couldn't take his eyes off her. He opened his mouth, he smacked his lips. He had taken a fancy to Cholchinay.

"Will you come into my yurt, girl?"

Cholchinay looked at him and laughed.

"Allykh, I am Choril's betrothed! When the sun stands shining next to me, how can I look at a toad?"

Allykh closed his mouth, wiped his lips.

"All right," he said. "We'll see how long your sun will shine!"

Allykh was going to make trouble.

Allykh was a shaman. Twelve brasses hung from his belt. Twelve shamans had worn this belt before him. Shaman Allykh had great powers.

One day Choril went hunting bear cubs. Cholchinay saw him off. Then she sat down to embroider her wedding robe.

Allykh took up his tambour, built a fire, and began to make magic, beating on his tambour and calling out the evil spirits. He made magic for a long time.

A strong wind blew over the snow. The snow whirled, stood up like a pillar, began to spin. A black storm cloud covered the sky. Out of the storm cloud a great wind came; it whirled all the snow into the air.

Darkness spread over everything. The blizzard was so thick that you couldn't see your own hand in front of you.

Never had there been such a blizzard. The Nivkhs' yurts were completely covered over by the snow. Where the village had been there was now only a smooth, white field. Where the forest had been now only the tops of pine trees poked through the snow.

Choril got caught in the blizzard.

He saw that there would be no hunting that day. He sniffed at the wind and knew it would blow for a long time. What should he do to save himself? Choril looked for an empty bear's lair. He didn't find an empty one; he found one with a she-bear in it. Choril told the she-bear that he hadn't come for her, but that the blizzard had driven him there. He lay down alongside the bear, got nice and warm, and then he fell asleep.

The blizzard howled for ten days and ten nights; it covered up the roads, knocked down trees, and whirled the snow as high as the sky. Then the wind quieted and the snow settled. It became very still. There was a frost, and a solid crust formed on top of the snow. Now was a good time for Choril to go after the bear cubs, but he couldn't wake up! Through his sleep he thought he heard the Master of the Mountain say to him, "Whoever sleeps through the winter with a she-bear in her lair becomes ours, a taiga person!" Choril tried to move; he wanted to get up and run out of the lair, but he didn't have the strength to throw off his sleep and wake up.

While Choril had been lying in the lair, fur had grown all over his body, and claws had grown on his hands and feet. Choril had become a taiga person, a bear.

Cholchinay waited for her bridegroom, but no bridegroom came.

The blizzard had quieted down. Day after day went by. It was time for Choril to return, and still he didn't come. Cholchinay cried; she pined for her Choril.

Allykh came to her and took her by the hand. "Why are you sitting by yourself, girl? Your bridegroom is not coming back. Come to my yurt."

Cholchinay tried to pull away, but Allykh was holding her hand so tightly that she couldn't get free. Cholchinay began to scream, calling for help. People came running.

Allykh said to them, "The girl has been left all alone. An evil demon has carried Choril off, and what will become of the girl now? I will take her into my yurt. I'm a kind man."

People were silent, afraid to say a word against Allykh. And Allykh dragged Cholchinay off to his yurt. He sat down on his bunk, scowled, and shook his finger at his women. His ten wives scurried about as fast as they could to prepare his food. They cut up some fishskin, melted some seal fat, and threw it all into the pot. They threw some berries and rice into the pot and cooked it all up. Then they crumbled some dried fish into it and added some white clay for color and flavor. When it was cooked, the wives chewed the food and put it into Allykh's mouth. All he had to do was to swallow it. Allykh offered some of his food to Cholchinay. "Eat!" he said. But Cholchinay didn't take any of Allykh's food. Instead, she chewed on some dried fish she had brought from home.

The winter was almost gone, and still Choril didn't come.

Every day Allykh asked Cholchinay, "Will you plait your hair into two braids soon, girl?"

"No, not soon," Cholchinay answered.

Cholchinay chose her time carefully. One night she dressed in hunting clothes and took a spear, the knife that Choril had made, her handbag that held her sewing, and a comb. She crept out of Allykh's house in the darkness to look for Choril.

Cholchinay walked along the taiga and noticed steam curling up out of a snowbank. She knew that meant that a bear's lair must be under the snowbank.

Cholchinay was tired and hungry. So she thought, "I'll awaken the bear and kill him. Who knows how much longer it will be before I find Choril? I'll kill the bear, I'll drink my fill of his hot blood, and it will make me stronger. And I'll take some of the meat along."

Cholchinay poked the spear into the thawed patch of ground and worried the bear in his lair with it.

The bear roared and climbed out of his lair. He was big, with fur shot through with silver. Cholchinay had never seen such a handsome bear. "What a good catch he is!" she thought. She stepped back and dug her heels harder into the ground. She raised her spear and aimed it at his heart in order to kill him quickly, so he wouldn't feel much pain. But the spear went off to one side and stuck in a snowbank; only the shaft was left swinging back and forth. Cholchinay grabbed her knife, drew her arm back, and struck hard at the bear's heart. But the knife curled up on itself and didn't even scratch the bear. At that Cholchinay closed her eyes, so as not to see her death coming.

But the bear said to her, "Don't be afraid, my Cholchinay. It is I—Choril."

"You are an evil demon!" cried Cholchinay. "You bewitched my knife and my spear!"

"No, Cholchinay," the bear said to her. "I made that knife and that spear myself. They still remember me, and that's why they couldn't harm me! I am Choril."

He told her all that had happened since last she had seen him. Then they realized that all this misfortune was the doing of Allykh, who wanted Cholchinay for his wife.

They sat down to think—what should they do? As long as Allykh was alive, Choril would remain a bear. But they mustn't kill Allykh, since he was of their own blood—and how could they spill their own blood? It would be a great sin. A sin like that is not forgiven.

Choril said, "Allykh has his own demon. If his demon is killed, Allykh will die. The demon dwells with the Master of the Mountain, in a pot near a post on top of a stone slab. The way there lies toward the sunset. But I cannot go. A live bear does not go to the Master of the Mountain. The road there is hard!"

Cholchinay thought a while and said, "I will go to the Master of the Mountain. I will kill that demon."

The bear rose and took the spear out of the snowbank, straightened the knife, and gave them both back to Cholchinay. They said good-bye, and Cholchinay started off toward the sunset.

Whether she walked for a long time, I do not know. Cholchinay did not count her steps; she did not stop on the way. She flew over the rivers on her spear. She flew over the mountains on her spear. She passed nine rivers. She passed nine lakes. She passed nine mountain peaks. She wasn't thinking of herself, she was thinking of Choril. Suddenly she saw a stone mountain whose summit disappeared into the clouds. It had neither ledges nor steps. Sheer rock rose from the earth straight up to the sky. It was solid stone! How was she to climb it?

Cholchinay took Choril's knife and threw it at the mountain. "Do your work, knife. Help me rescue your master from his misfortune!"

The knife drove itself into the stone. Sparks flew in all directions as the knife started to chisel the stone, carving out steps.

Cholchinay began to climb the steps. Meanwhile the sun went into his yurt to sleep; the sky people kindled the lights in the night sky, and Chol-

chinay kept climbing up the mountain. She wasn't thinking of herself—she was thinking of Choril, of his misfortune, as she kept climbing the mountain.

The sun awoke and opened the door of his yurt. The sky people extinguished the lights of the night. And Cholchinay was still climbing the mountain. The knife jumped ahead of her, striking the stone; sparks were scattering in all directions, and Cholchinay kept climbing, step by step. She wasn't looking down, she wasn't thinking about herself.

Cholchinay stepped onto the last step. She sharpened her knife on the stone and put it away in its case. She looked down—and almost fell! The earth was so far below her that rivers stretched like little threads and the hills looked like sable droppings.

Cholchinay went still farther.

She saw a tall house: its logs were made of stone, its posts of iron. The house was so tall that no matter how she craned her neck, she could not see the roof.

A serpent with scales of stone lay before the door. Cholchinay could see only his head, as his body was lost in fog. That's how big the serpent was! He was looking at Cholchinay with his green eyes, staring without ever blinking.

A cold chill gripped Cholchinay's knees and started moving up her legs; her hands grew weak. How would she manage him?

Then Cholchinay's handbag came to life and began to move. Out of it Cholchinay took a needle made of bone with a thread made of sinew and threw them in the serpent's eyes.

The needle started shuttling in and out of the serpent's eyes, now up, now down—now piercing the upper lid, now the lower, pulling the thread after it. Before the chill had reached Cholchinay's waist, the needle had already sewn one of the serpent's eyes shut and was starting on the other. The serpent shook his head back and forth; he couldn't understand what was happening, why his eyes were closing.

The bone needle sewed the serpent's second eye closed, and at once the chill left Cholchinay. Now she could move her feet, and she ran up to the door. The door opened itself before her.

Beyond the door was another door. In front of this door lay a big lizard. Cholchinay had never seen a lizard like this before. He was made all of iron, his black jaws were open, and a forked tongue quivered inside his mouth. The lizard blew on Cholchinay, and her legs sank into the earth up to her knees.

Cholchinay took the thimble from her handbag, threw it, and got it right in the lizard's mouth, where it plugged up his throat. The lizard tried to blow on Cholchinay again, but he couldn't. Cholchinay pulled her legs out of the ground and ran up to the door. The door opened itself before her.

Beyond that door was a third door. A tiger guarded it. He bared his teeth, and his teeth were as long as your forearm. He beat the ground with his tail, and his tail was as thick as a larch-tree trunk. Cholchinay threw her comb into the tiger's mouth. The comb lodged itself across the tiger's throat and wouldn't budge. The wider the tiger opened his mouth, the longer the comb's teeth became. The tiger roared, but he couldn't do anything to Cholchinay. She saw that the tiger was too busy to bother her, so she stepped up to the door, and the door opened itself before her.

Beyond that door was the Master's yurt. Everything in that yurt was the same as in ordinary people's homes, except that there were stars on the ceiling and a sun in every window. On the floor near the bunk lay more animal skins than you could count. The Master put the souls of killed animals into these skins, so that the animals would not vanish from the earth no matter how many of them were killed by hunters.

Cholchinay looked around. She saw that the ceiling was held up by posts. Near one post lay a stone slab; on the slab stood a pot.

An old man was sitting on the bunk; his face was radiant.

Cholchinay realized that this was the Master of the Mountain himself. She got down on her knees, folded her hands, and asked him to hear her tale. She told of her misfortune and why she had come.

The Master said to her, "Of course I know Choril! He was a good hunter, did everything according to law—did not pour water into the campfire, did not cut the bear with a sword, did not break the bear's bones. It's bad that such misfortune has befallen him! Look into that pot—many shamans' demons live there. Which one is Allykh's, I don't know. You are a brave girl, you have borne much sorrow. Take what you came for. Go up to the pot and shout, 'Allykh's demon, go to serve your master!' and when it comes out, grab it."

And Cholchinay did as she was told.

No sooner did she shout, "Allykh's demon, go to serve your master!" than a black worm jumped out of the pot. Cholchinay grabbed it with her hand, held it tight in her fist, and ran.

She came to the edge of the mountain, climbed astride her spear, and leaped down. She flew, with the wind whistling in her ears, crags and boulders rushing by! The spear flew, with Cholchinay holding onto it with both hands. The spear flew over mountains and forests, over lakes and rivers.

At last the spear reached the place where Choril was waiting for his betrothed. Cholchinay got off the spear and went up to Choril.

Choril said, "To whom will I leave my bearskin?"

"Someone will turn up," said Cholchinay.

Just then she saw Allykh running toward them.

When Allykh saw Cholchinay, he shouted, "So that's where you are, worthless girl! What a time I had finding you!"

"You shouldn't have bothered looking for me," said Cholchinay. "You looked for me, but instead you have found your fate."

Then she threw down the demon she had been holding in her fist. She stepped on it and crushed it.

Allykh began to reel and stumble. He got down on all fours. Then the bearskin slid off Choril, jumped onto the shaman, and wrapped itself around him. Allykh became a bear. It served him right! Why did he wish harm to Choril and Cholchinay? Cholchinay raised her spear at him. This frightened Allykh, and he fled into the taiga.

Choril and Cholchinay took each other by the hand and started for home. On the way Cholchinay plaited her hair into two braids.

They married. They lived a long life, and until their last day they loved each other very much.

People treasure what comes hard.

The Strongest in the World

One winter's day, when the Amur River was frozen solid, some Nanai children ran outdoors to skate on the ice.

At first they played and skated, but soon they began to fight. One boy, Nameka, hit another boy, Kurbu, and knocked him down. He then began to boast, "I beat Kurbu! I am the strongest one here. You must all bow before me!"

Just as he said that, Nameka slipped on the ice, fell hard, and struck the back of his head.

"See," Kurbu said to him, "you're not the strongest. Ice is stronger than you are—Ice beat you. Look! Your head is bleeding. You must bow before Ice."

Nameka asked the ice, "Listen, Ice, is there anyone stronger than you?"

"Yes," answered Ice. "Sun is stronger than I am. As soon as he begins to warm me, I melt. Bow before Sun."

The boys set out toward the sun. They walked a long way. Finally they came to the sun. "Listen, Father Sun," said Nameka, "I beat Kurbu, Ice beat me, you can melt Ice, so you are stronger than we are. I have come to bow before you."

Sun thought a while, thought some more, then answered, "Storm Cloud is stronger than I am. When she covers the earth, it turns cold; my rays cannot pierce Storm Cloud."

So the boys set off to find the storm cloud. They climbed a high mountain. All about them was fog, dampness, and cold. By the time they reached Storm Cloud, they were tired and wet and coated with frost.

"Listen, Mother Storm Cloud," called Nameka. "I am stronger than Kurbu, Ice is stronger than I am, Sun is stronger than Ice, you are stronger than Sun—so you must be the strongest of all. I have come to bow before you."

Just as the storm cloud was about to answer, the wind began to blow. It whirled and whistled and whirred, and it scattered the storm cloud. Only a moment ago it had been cold and damp and so dark one could not see anything two steps away. Suddenly it became warm and bright: the sun shone, a rainbow appeared, and all of the Amur River from its headwaters to its mouth became as clear to see as the palm of your hand.

At this sight Nameka shouted to the wind, "Listen, Wind! I beat Kurbu, Ice cracked the back of my head, Sun melted Ice, Storm Cloud covered Sun, and you chased away Storm Cloud. So you are the strongest of us all. I bow before you!"

Nameka bowed.

Then Kurbu asked Wind, "Can you move the mountain from its place?"

Wind began to blow. But no matter how hard it blew, puffing out its cheeks, the mountain stood in its place as before. Only little grains of sand flew off its top.

"Well," said Nameka to Wind. "You'll need a lot of time to move the mountain from one place to another. So Mountain is stronger than you are." And both boys bowed before Mountain.

"Mountain—oh, Mountain," asked Nameka, "are you the strongest in the world?"

Mountain grunted and thought a while. "No," it said. "Tree is stronger than I. It grows on my back and tears me apart with its roots. It even protects me from Wind."

Nameka bowed before Tree. "Listen, Tree!" he said, "I beat Kurbu, Ice beat me, Sun beat Ice, Storm Cloud beat Sun, Wind beat Storm Cloud, Mountain beat Wind, and you can beat Mountain. Are you the strongest of all?"

The tree rustled its leaves. "Yes," it said, "I am the strongest of all."

"No, you are wrong," Nameka answered. And he took an ax and chopped down the tree.

Then everyone bowed before Nameka: Mountain, Wind, Storm Cloud, Sun, and Ice.

And from that time on it was agreed that Man is the strongest in the world.

Ayoga

There once lived a Nanai of the Samarov clan named La. He had a daughter named Ayoga. She was a beautiful girl, and everybody loved her. One day somebody said that there was no one more beautiful than La's daughter—not in this village, nor in any other. Ayoga flushed with pride and examined her face very carefully. She liked what she saw.

After that Ayoga looked at herself all the time. She would gaze at her face and could not tear herself away; she would stare at her face and could not look at herself enough. She looked at her image in the shiny copper basin and looked at her reflection in the water.

She stopped doing anything else at all. She just kept admiring herself. She became very lazy.

One day her mother said to her, "Go bring some water, Ayoga!"

Ayoga answered, "I'll fall in the water."

"Hold onto a bush."

"A bush will break."

"Grab onto a strong bush."

"I'll scratch my hands."

"Put on mittens."

"They will tear." Ayoga kept looking at herself in the copper basin. Oh, how beautiful she was!

"Sew the mittens up with a needle," said her mother.

"The needle will break."

"Use a thick needle," said her father.

"I'll prick my finger," answered the daughter.

"Put on a thimble made of leather."

"The thimble will break."

Ayoga didn't budge from her place.

A neighbor girl came by and said, "I'll go get the water, mother." The girl went to the river and brought water—as much as they needed.

Then the mother kneaded some dough and made bird-cherry cakes. She baked them on a blazing hearth.

Ayoga saw them and called out, "Give me a cake, mother!"

"It's hot—you'll burn your hands," the mother answered.

"I'll put on mittens," said Ayoga.

"The mittens are wet."

"I'll dry them in the sun."

"They'll stiffen in the sun."

"I'll soften them with the brake."

"Your hands will hurt," said the mother. "Why should you work and spoil your beauty? It would be better to give a cake to a girl who doesn't have to worry about her hands."

And so the mother gave a cake to the neighbor girl.

Ayoga became angry. She went down to the river where she could admire her reflection in the water. And the neighbor girl sat on the riverbank, munching the bird-cherry cake.

Ayoga kept turning to look at the girl, and her neck began to stretch. It became very, very long.

Finally the girl said to Ayoga, "Go ahead and take the cake, Ayoga. I don't mind."

Then Ayoga got really angry. She started flapping her arms at the girl, she spread her fingers wide, she turned white with rage. How could she, a beauty, eat a cake that had already been bitten into! She flapped her arms so hard that they changed into wings.

"I don't want anything! You can just go-go-go!" screamed Ayoga.

She lost her foothold on the bank, tumbled into the water, and instantly changed into a goose. She swam around, and as she swam she screamed, "Oh, how beautiful I am! Go-go-go! Oh, how beautiful I am! Ga-ga-ga!"

She swam and she swam, until she forgot how to speak the Nanai language. She forgot every word.

She remembered only her name, in order that she, a beauty, would not be mistaken for anyone else. And to this day, as soon as she sees a human being, she screams, "Ay-oga-ga-ga! Ay-oga-ga-ga!"

Seven Fears

All these things happened when the Udege still believed that they saw a stone man when they looked at a stone, saw a taiga man when they looked at a bear, saw a water man when they looked at a fish, saw a tree man when they looked at a tree. All kinds of things happened to people then—things that don't happen today.

Two brothers—Solomdiga and Indiga—lived along the headwaters of the River Koppi.

When their father lay dying, he told them on his deathbed, "Stand up for each other. If one of you is in trouble, the other must help. And both of you should always look straight ahead. This do I tell you, and this you must do."

The father died. The brothers braided white ribbons in their hair. They laid the father in a coffin. They placed the coffin with the father's feet toward the east, so that even after death he could see the sun rise. For seven days they carried food to him—to feed his soul.

Then they went hunting.

"Both of you should always look straight ahead," the father had said to the brothers. But the younger, Indiga, walking behind his brother, kept looking every which way; he was very sharp-eyed and did not like looking always at the same spot.

The brothers walked and walked. Indiga kept looking every which way. Suddenly he heard a noise. He turned—he saw a tiger jumping out of the underbrush on the forest floor, straight at his older brother! Solomdiga did not have time to aim his spear or to take out his knife. Indiga, being farther off, should have thrown a spear at the tiger. But he was afraid, and his heart became the heart of a hare. He fell to the ground, pressed his palms together, and begged the tiger to pass by without touching him or his brother.

Indiga lay that way for a long time. Then he lifted his head and looked—neither the tiger nor his brother was to be seen. Both had vanished. Indiga's heart began to ache. He began to call his brother. He shouted and shouted, but no one answered; only the hills mockingly echoed his cry: "So-lo-om! Di-di! Ga-ga! A-a-a!"

Indiga began to cry. How would he live without his brother? What would he tell his kinsmen? How would he wipe the shame off his face?

He cried and cried, but there was no getting out of it. Mother was waiting, so he had to hunt and bring home some game.

Indiga looked at his traps. A polecat was caught in one of them. As soon as he saw Indiga, he began to shout at him, "Go away, you who have lost your brother!" He bit through the leg caught in the trap and bounded off on three legs.

Indiga looked at his snares. A weasel was caught in a noose. The weasel saw Indiga and began to shout, "It is disgusting to be caught by someone like you! You lost your brother!" He tore the noose and ran off into the taiga.

Indiga shot an arrow at a goose. The arrow flew up and struck the goose under her wing. But the goose pulled the arrow out with her beak, threw it back at Indiga, and shouted, "How could I be the catch of someone like you? You lost your brother, Indiga-ga!"

Then the goose flew to the middle of the river, folded her wings, threw herself in the water, and drowned.

Neither beasts nor birds would allow themselves to be caught by a man with the heart of a hare.

Indiga sat down and started to think. He thought for a long time. He smoked up all his tobacco; he smoked up all the moss around him. His heart ached. Indiga thought, "I lost my brother. It's a bad thing to lose your brother. Your heart aches. Even if you only lose your pipe, you don't rest until you find it! And I lost my brother . . . I'll go look for Solomdiga. If I find him, my heart will stop aching. And if I get lost myself, my heart will stop aching also!"

Indiga went to his mother. He fell on his knees. He told her everything. He told her how his heart had become the heart of a hare. His mother kissed him. She said to him, weeping, "Father taught you to look straight ahead. You didn't listen, you lost your brother, you found the heart of a hare. Go look for a man's heart. Go look for your brother. He was lost because of your fear. You will bring him back now only with courage!"

Indiga took a pipe, a flint, a knife, and a spear. He started off. But he didn't know where to go. He walked toward the sunset.

He met a crawling grass snake. He asked him where to look for his brother. The grass snake didn't know. Indiga went on.

He met a mouse running along the ground. He asked whether she had seen Solomdiga. The mouse hadn't seen him. Indiga went on.

He saw a squirrel climbing the trees. He asked her. No, the squirrel hadn't seen his brother.

He came to a river. He saw fish swimming in the water. He asked the fish—had they seen Solomdiga? The fish hadn't seen him. Indiga went on.

He saw a jumping toad. The toad hadn't seen him.

He saw a flying warbler. He asked her. The warbler answered that she had not seen Solomdiga—that she flew too low.

He asked a crane, who flies higher. The crane hadn't seen him, either. The crane said, "Ask the eagle, who flies the highest of all."

Indiga asked the eagle whether he had seen where the tiger had taken his brother Solomdiga.

The eagle said, "Your brother is far, far away. You will find him if you overcome seven fears. You have the heart of a hare now. When you have

67

a brave man's heart you will find your brother." The eagle threw down one of his feathers and said, "I will help you. Where my feather flies, there you must go!"

The feather flew toward the sunset. Indiga followed it.

Whether he walked a long time, I do not know. He crossed three brooks. The feather flew on in front of him. Indiga looked straight ahead, as his father had taught. Indiga, who had lost his brother, walked on.

He came to a river. The eagle's feather flew above the river. Indiga built a boat and put it into the water. The river began to foam, to seethe, to bubble; the water boiled as if in a caldron. Steam rose up from the water. Fog spread out through the valleys. Indiga's boat shriveled, buckled, and sank. The fish in the river got cooked, and they floated with their bellies up, looking at Indiga with white eyes. Indiga became frightened, but he had to go on, or else he would have the heart of a hare forever. He said to himself, "This is not fear yet. Fear is still ahead."

Indiga set up his bow between two trees. He drew the bowstring and fastened it to a branch to keep it taut. Then he put an arrow onto the bow. He gripped the arrow with one hand and broke the branch with the other. The branch cracked off, the bowstring snapped back, the bow unbent, and the arrow went flying. It flew above the boiling river, carrying Indiga with it. The steam swirled around him and scalded him, but he endured it. The river was wide. While flying across it, his body became scalded all over. "I don't mind," said Indiga. "It will heal."

The arrow came down on the opposite shore. Indiga got to his feet. He saw the eagle's feather waiting for him. No sooner was he on the ground than the feather flew on. Indiga followed.

He walked and he walked. He jumped over three brooks, he climbed over three hills. Between two hills he saw a rocky clearing. A narrow path led to the clearing. The path was strewn with bones and edged with skulls. Indiga grew frightened. But the eagle's feather flew along the path, straight at the rocky clearing. Indiga saw a tiger camp in the clearing. There were as many tigers there as bees in a hive! They were tearing their prey to pieces. They were fondling each other, fighting each other. They roared so loud the roar was like the sound of thunder over Agdy's camp.

The eagle's feather flew above the tiger camp.

Indiga's heart was beating fast. "They'll eat me up!" he thought.

In this, his last hour, he sat down to smoke his pipe. That reminded

him of his flint. He pulled some dry grass out of his tinderbox and twisted it into a braid. He put the braid on his head. He struck a fire and lighted the braid.

The dry grass on Indiga's head blazed like a campfire. Indiga dashed through the tiger camp. The tigers scattered in all directions. They saw nothing but the fire—they did not see Indiga! The tigers roared, beat the ground with their tails, and opened their red mouths wide. Indiga ran past them. He kept saying to himself, "This is not fear yet. Fear is still ahead." Indiga passed through the tiger camp and left it behind. But not until he had killed a tiger, and drunk its blood, and taken some meat and the tiger skin with him.

The eagle's feather was flying in front of Indiga again. No sooner had he finished with the tiger than it flew on. It didn't look for roads, it flew in a straight line. Indiga jumped over three brooks, climbed over three hills, crossed three rivers. Beyond the last river a forest began.

In that forest the trees were as high as the sky. They were so dense that the sun's rays could not penetrate the branches; the wind could not force its way through the branches. The trees were laced together with vines. Their branches twisted themselves and grabbed, like hands. They would let an animal through, but not a human being. Indiga saw white bones glistening among the tree branches. He grew frightened. His heart was pounding, his hands were shaking, but he said to himself, "This is not fear yet. Fear is still ahead." He pulled the tiger skin over himself, cut the meat into pieces, and put them on his spear. Then he entered the forest.

The trees smelled the meat and reached for Indiga. With their branch hands they felt Indiga all over. As soon as a branch tried to touch him, Indiga would throw it a piece of meat. The trees started to snatch the meat away from each other. They began to fight over the meat. They lashed each other with their branches—bark and chips flew in all directions. Indiga walked farther and farther through the forest, following the eagle's feather. He gathered some branches from the trees and took them along, thinking, "I'll build a campfire when I can."

The eagle's feather flew on. Indiga jumped over six brooks, climbed over six hills, crossed six rivers.

He came to a swamp. The feather flew above it. What should Indiga do? He threw the tree branches on the swamp and walked on the branches. The branches barely floated on top of the swamp water. The swamp was bubbling. Blue lights were flitting over it. Indiga came to the middle of the swamp. A little hunchbacked man stood in his way. The man had one leg and one arm.

Indiga grew frightened. His heart began to beat fast, his hands and feet began to shake. Indiga recognized the little man, even though he had never seen him. The man was called Boko. He did only harm to people. He led them around a swamp until they were sucked into the quagmire.

Boko said, "Where are you going, fellow?"

"I am looking for you," answered Indiga. What had he to lose?

"Here I am," said Boko. "What do you want from me?"

"I heard," said Indiga, "that your one leg is stronger than any two. I cannot believe this. So I have come to see for myself. Let's see who can jump higher. Where I come from, nobody can jump higher than I."

"You jump first, then," said Boko.

Indiga jumped. He jumped higher than a tree. He came down, spread his legs, and landed on the branches. He sank into the swamp up to his waist. But the branches did not let him drown.

Boko laughed. "Is that any way to jump?" he asked. "This is the way!"

He squatted down on his one leg, straightened it, and gave such a huge jump that he flew up to the clouds. Then he turned himself head down and flew back.

But Indiga walked on, picking up branches from behind him and laying them ahead, walking out of the swamp.

When Boko came down, his whole body went into the quagmire. While he was getting himself out and rubbing his eyes, Indiga climbed onto solid ground. He was standing in a clear spot. Boko did not frighten him any more.

Indiga said to himself, "That was not fear yet. Fear is still ahead."

Boko shouted to Indiga, "Hey, fellow, did you see how one should jump? Come here!"

"No time!" Indiga shouted back. "I have business to attend to."

The eagle's feather was flying on. Indiga didn't have time to dry himself off—he simply went on, covered with mud.

He jumped over nine brooks, he climbed over nine hills. He had torn his boots so badly he was walking barefoot, bruising his feet. He crossed nine lakes.

A large serpent crawled out of the ninth lake, twisting himself into rings. His scales were made of stone; they were shiny, and they rattled. A flame blazed from his mouth. The ground and the grass under him were burning. The serpent breathed on Indiga, scorching his clothes and singeing his eyebrows.

Indiga grew frightened. He paled, his heart beat fast, his hands and feet shook, his forehead was covered with sweat. But he reassured himself, "This is not fear yet. Fear is still ahead." He gathered up his courage and shouted to the serpent, "Hey, if you want to eat me up, here is a piece of fat! Maybe one piece will be enough for you."

He picked up a stone from the ground, scraped some dirt off his body, covered the stone with it, and threw the stone into the serpent's mouth.

The serpent choked. He couldn't swallow the stone, and he couldn't breathe fire on Indiga.

While the serpent was busy with the stone, Indiga ran off.

And the eagle's feather kept flying in a straight line; it didn't look for roads.

Indiga jumped over nine brooks, climbed over nine hills, crossed nine lakes and nine forests. He was walking barefoot; the stones rubbed the skin off his feet almost down to the flesh. He came to a rocky gorge.

Now he was the most frightened of all: scattered all around were living stones! They turned and looked after him as he passed; they rolled and talked to each other in stone language. But the feather flew on. Indiga followed it.

Suddenly Indiga saw a man standing among the stones. He was so tall that you had to crane your neck to see his face. Indiga had never seen a man like that, but he knew at once who was standing before him: Kakzamu—the evil mountain man. Indiga turned white, his heart beat fast, his hands and feet shook, and his hair stood on end from fright. But he said to himself, "This is not fear yet. Fear is still ahead." He bowed to Kakzamu.

Kakzamu asked him, "What are you doing here?"

Considering himself lost anyway, Indiga said to him, "Neighbor, they say you have great power!"

"They tell the truth," answered Kakzamu. "Do you see all those stones lying around? Those were all people, but I turned them into stones, to guard my hills and everything under them. Now I'll turn you into stone too!"

He touched Indiga's hand, and the hand turned to stone. Indiga couldn't move his hand or raise it. His hand became black. Indiga nearly died with fear.

But he gathered up his courage and said, "Eh, my grandfather could do this! That's not such a great power—to turn living flesh into stone. Let's see you turn stone into living flesh! My grandfather could, but he died a long time ago. Now nobody can do it."

74

Kakzamu answered Indiga, "My power is at my command; whatever I want to do, I will do!"

He touched Indiga's hand. The hand became alive again. Warm blood began to run through it, and it began to move.

"That's not all!" shouted Indiga. "Come here, bend down to me, and I'll whisper in your ear what my grandfather knew but carried off with him when he died."

The mountain man bent down to Indiga. He turned his ear toward him. He rolled his eyes. His nostrils were so large that a whole fist could fit into one. Indiga pulled his tobacco pouch from inside his belt and poured all the tobacco into Kakzamu's nose.

Kakzamu began to sneeze. He sneezed and sneezed and sneezed. All his power left him through his nose, and only after some time could more power come to him. Indiga started to run—away from Kakzamu.

Again he followed the eagle's feather. He jumped over a brook, climbed over three hills, circled six lakes, crossed nine forests. His feet were rubbed down to the bone.

Indiga walked and walked, and then he saw a stone wall standing before him. You couldn't walk around that wall, and you couldn't climb over it. To the left and to the right, the wall stretched from one end of the earth to the other; its top was in the clouds.

The eagle's feather struck the wall and scattered into dust, as though it had never existed.

Now Indiga became really frightened, so frightened that words cannot describe it. The wall could not be conquered by strength. The wall could not be conquered by cunning. Indiga looked at himself and began to cry. His feet were rubbed to the bone. His hands were burned. His clothes were in rags. His belly was sticking to his back from hunger. Indiga had overcome many fears, but his brother was nowhere in sight! Indiga took out his knife and said, "I will not turn back. None of my kinfolk ever turned back. I'll cut out my hare's heart. I will wipe the shame off my face."

He put the knife to his breast. Suddenly, a door appeared in the wall. What other fear lay behind it?

Indiga overcame his fear: "How can I be afraid? I am a man!"

At once he heard in his breast the beating of a man's heart. He took his spear in his hand. He struck the door with the spear, with all his might. The door flew open. Indiga leaped through the door, ready for anything.

But what was this?

He saw that he was standing on the same spot where he had lost his brother. And there wasn't any wall there at all!

Scattered about were day lilies, burning with an orange flame, and there were birds chirping.

And right in front of Indiga stood his brother Solomdiga. He was holding a beautiful girl by the hand. Indiga had never seen a girl so beautiful. Her eyelashes were like rushes; her eyes were yellow and shining like the sun. The girl was wearing a yellow wedding robe. On the robe were black stripes, as on a tiger skin.

Solomdiga said, "Thank you, brother! For my sake you did not let anything frighten you!"

The girl smiled at Indiga and said, "I am a tiger person. I fell in love with your brother. That's why I carried him off to my land. But I saw that you could not live without your brother. So I begged the Master of Tigers to let me join people. Now I will live with you. I can live among you—you are a brave people!"

They took one another by the hand, and the three of them started off together.

They made their mother very happy.

Solomdiga and the tiger girl became husband and wife.

And Indiga learned to look straight ahead. He never had the heart of a hare again.

The Braggart

If you believe a braggart, you'll get into trouble.

A hare once lived in the taiga. He looked like any other hare: long ears, two short legs to hold food, two long legs to run away from enemies. But this hare was a braggart. The other hares had never seen a braggart like him.

One day the hare ate a small day-lily root. Then he told the other hares, "I was running in the forest, looking for food. Suddenly I banged into something so hard that I almost broke my head. See how I tore my lip!"

The other hares laughed. "Yes, it's true, your lip is forked. But all hares have lips like that."

The hare answered, "All hares may have lips like that, but mine is special. If you want to hear, don't interrupt. I banged myself and saw a day lily the like of which no one has ever seen. Its stem was as high as a larch! Its flower was enormous! Its root was the size of a bear! I started to dig for it. My teeth are sharp. My paws are strong. I piled up two mounds of earth, one on each side of the day lily. I dug out the root. I dug out a root so big that I ate it for ten whole days without finishing even half of it. Look how fat I got!"

The hares looked. "You are like the rest of us," they said. "No fatter than other hares."

"I got smaller," the braggart answered, "because I ran back fast—I wanted to show you the root. I am generous! I had enough to eat for my whole life—but I thought, let my brothers eat some of the root, which is sweeter than any root they have ever eaten."

What hare would refuse a sweet root! The other hares' mouths began to water. They asked, "And how will we find the way there?"

"I'll show you," the hare said. "I don't mind."

The hares followed the braggart. They came to a clearing.

The braggart said, "Here is where I saw a day lily as high as a larch. Here is where I piled up two mounds of earth with my paws."

"Where are the mounds?" the other hares asked the braggart.

"The river has carried them away."

"Where is the river?"

"It has flowed out to sea."

"Where is the day lily?"

"It has withered; I gnawed off its root."

"And where is the day-lily's stem?"

"A badger has eaten it."

"Where is the badger?"

"He's gone off into the taiga."

"Where is the taiga?"

"A fire has burned it."

"Where are the ashes?"

"The wind has scattered them."

"Where are the stumps?"

"They're covered with grass."

The hares sat back and looked blank; they couldn't figure it out—were things the way the hare had told it, or not?

The braggart kept on. "It's not hard to find such a day lily! It's a simple thing to find such a day lily. All you have to do is run straight but look to the sides. You'll see it—if not on one side, then on the other . . ."

The hares dashed off in all directions. They flew across the ground, their eyes looking sideways in both directions. They could see their tails—but what was ahead of them, that they could not see. They forced their eyes to look in opposite directions because they were afraid they'd miss the sweet day lily as high as a larch. They ran and ran, until they got so tired they fell right off their feet. By that time they were so hungry that ordinary grass seemed to them sweeter than day lilies.

To this day they cannot bring their eyes together. Thanks to the braggart, all hares are walleyed.

79

The Poor Man Monokto

A good job is never wasted. It will always be useful—if not for you, for your son; if not for your son, for your grandson.

The old father of a young Ulch man was dying. On his deathbed, he called his son to him, looked at him, and began to weep. "I feel sorry for you, son! My grandfather was an angaza—a poor man. My father was an angaza, they called me angaza my whole life, and now it looks as though you will have to be an angaza too. I worked my whole life for the rich man Bolda, and I've earned nothing. Bolda has a light hand when he takes; Bolda has a heavy hand when he gives. I have nothing to leave you—only a knife, a flint, and a fish spear. They were left to me by my father; my father got them from my grandfather. Now let them serve you!''

The father spoke, and then he died.

They dressed him for his last journey. They buried him. They held a small wake.

Monokto took the knife, the flint, and the fish spear and began to work for Bolda, as his father had done.

And the people forgot his name. Instead, they called him angaza—poor man.

The old man had been right—Bolda had a heavy hand when he gave.

One day Bolda called in the young man Monokto and said to him, ''Your father owed me a debt; the debt has now been transferred to you. If you do not work off your father's debt, the shaman will not take his soul to Buni. But I will help you—I will feed and clothe you. I will keep an account of the food you eat up and of the clothes you wear out.''

Monokto started working off his father's debt, and Bolda started helping him. But every day this help made it worse for the poor man. Monokto wore other people's castoffs, he ate other people's leavings, and he didn't dare complain.

Bolda could hardly open his mouth, his face was so fat, but he said, ''Work, Monokto, work! You and I are like brothers now. We are both helping your father's soul enter Buni—I, by giving you work, and you, by working. Work, Monokto!''

Riches came to Bolda from all over. He was friendly with the merchants across the sea; he bought goods from them, and he sold the goods to his kinsmen for triple the price. Half the village worked for him—they caught fish and dried them for him, and they looked after his dogs. Half the village worked for him in the taiga—there they hunted animals and birds. Bolda took everything home. He had ten wives—he had taken them all from his kinsmen for debts and hadn't paid a bride price for any of them. Bolda had ten bondsmen—they were working off their debts, cursing their bitter lives. Every autumn Bolda sailed to the Chinese kingdom in ten boats with yellow sails of fishskin. In the city of San-Sing, the headman himself drank tea with Bolda and bought furs from the rich man; he did not ask Bolda how much he had paid for the pelts, but gave him a good price.

The fat on Bolda's body kept getting thicker and thicker. Every day he grew heavier, while Monokto grew thin and was so hungry he could hardly drag his feet.

One day Monokto said to Bolda, "Let me fish a little for myself! You see—my belly is stuck to my back. I will die—and then how will I work off my father's debt?"

Bolda said with a kind voice, "All right, go ahead and fish! But first fish for my big tank, then for yourself. And don't take my fish spear! Don't touch my boat!"

Monokto fished a whole day before he filled Bolda's tank. Then it began to rain. It poured! The angaza sat down on the riverbank—how was he to fish for himself? He had no boat. He had no strength. He picked up his father's fish spear, but he could not throw it. He looked at his hands and began to weep. "This is the end of me, death is coming for me, my hands are drying up!" He looked at the things his father had left him—the knife, the fish spear, and the flint—and he became angry. "You are bad helpers to me. How many years have you been working? It's about time you learned to do things by yourselves! Without my hands you aren't good for anything!"

The knife grew ashamed. It came to life at Monokto's belt and began to move. It jumped out of its case and ran into the forest. It cut down dead trees—it piled up a whole mountain of wood! It cut willow branches for a tent—it cut a whole pile!

The flint looked at its master. Monokto was lying down, not stirring. The flint jumped out of its little bag, jumped up to the pile of dead trees, struck a light, and kindled a campfire.

In the meantime the knife had built a tent. Then it ran off into the taiga again. It felled a big poplar. It hollowed out a boat. The shavings were curling into rings, flying off in all directions, and the log was grunting and rolling, first turning one side to the knife, then the other.

Before Monokto could blink his eyes, his father's knife had made him a boat, such as no master builder ever had made before.

Monokto went into the tent. He sat down. He stretched his hands to the fire. He began to warm them so he could start working with the fish spear.

Then the fish spear came to life and began to move. It was ashamed that its companions were working while it was lying idle. It got up and launched the boat with a shove of its shaft; the boat glided onto the river. The flint jumped into the boat and struck a light—the light attracted fish. Then the fish spear went

to work. Each time it struck the water, it pulled out a salmon, a sturgeon, or a carp.

The boat came back to shore. The fish spear leaned against the tent. The flint went back into its little bag.

Monokto ate his fill. He felt that he was getting his strength back, that he was becoming a man again. And the knife, having done its work, jumped back into its case at Monokto's belt.

Monokto said to his tools, "Thank you! Now I see you are good helpers. With your help I will work off my father's debt. Then I will fish for myself. I'll be able to stop worrying about Bolda."

But Bolda—suddenly there he was. He had seen a light on the river, heard the fish splashing, smelled the fish frying, and he couldn't stand it—he had to find out who, without his knowledge, was making a campfire, catching fish, and eating fried fish. He came running. He saw his angaza sitting by the fire. He had eaten his fill. There was a roomy tent over him and a big fire in front of the tent. And a new boat was standing at the shore, filled with fish.

"Eh!" said Bolda. "What is this, angaza? You cannot work off your father's debt, but look what a big catch you have! You say you have no strength, but see what a tent you've made! And why did you take my boat?"

"It's not your boat," the angaza Monokto answered.

"It's not yours, either. You don't have a boat," said Bolda.

"Yes, it's mine," answered Monokto.

He told Bolda how his old father's tools had helped him when he felt he was about to die.

Bolda looked at the young man. He spoke to him in a quiet voice. "That's good, angaza! I'll forgive you your father's debt, if you will give me your knife."

Monokto became sad. He thought a while. He smoked a while. He decided he had to give up his knife. He gave his knife to Bolda. But Bolda didn't leave. Again he spoke in a kind voice. "I forgave you your father's big debt. But he owed me a middle-sized debt too. There is a notch on the wall in my middle-sized storehouse. Give me your fish spear!"

Monokto sighed. He gave Bolda his fish spear. But Bolda still sat there. He smoked a while and then spoke in a sweet voice. "Angaza, your father also owed me a little debt—on the wall of my little storehouse there is a notch too. Give me your flint! Then your father's record will be clean. And what you yourself owe, I'll take from you later."

84

Monokto began to weep. He gave Bolda his flint.

Bolda ran off. In one hand he held the old man's things, in the other his fat belly, so it wouldn't get in the way when he ran.

"Never mind," thought Monokto. "I lifted a big load off myself—my father's debt. Now it will be easier for me!"

Bolda got up the next morning. He was happy because the old man's things would work for him now—and he wouldn't have to feed them.

Bolda went into the forest. Poor men were working for him there—they were building a boat, hollowing it out of a poplar log. Bolda started pushing them around, shouting, "Why are you working so badly! I am not going to feed you! One knife by itself will make everything faster for me than all of you, lazy men! This knife built a boat for Monokto in the time he took to smoke one pipe."

Bolda took the knife out of its case and threw it into the forest. The knife fell and did not move. It would not go to cut down the trees. It would not go to build a boat.

"What is this?" said Bolda. "The knife worked for Monokto by itself."

The people looked at the rich man and said, "Monokto's hands know how to do everything, that's why the knife listened to him. Your hands know only how to collect money and count it."

Bolda ran to the river. He grabbed the fish spear and threw it into the river. The fish spear sank in the water and stuck on the bottom of the river. Bolda could not pull it out, no matter how hard he tried.

Bolda got angry. He saw that the old man's tools did not want to serve him. He pulled the flint out of the bag and threw it on the ground. The flint struck the ground and sparked a fire. The fire ran along the ground—it came to Bolda's house and to his storehouses. Before Bolda could blink his eye, the fire began to play all over the storehouses and the house. The rich man's goods caught on fire.

Bolda threw himself at the fire. He wanted to stomp it out, but he couldn't. He got so hot from the fire that all the fat on his body melted.

And Bolda melted away. All that was left of him was his boots and his robe.

Monokto went to the spot where the rich man had thrown his knife. He saw that the knife had sunk into the rocks. They had become iron rocks. If you crushed them and smelted them in a fire, iron would pour out.

Monokto went to get his fish spear. He grabbed it with his hand, and he saw that green shoots had appeared on it—a tree was growing out of the fish spear.

The Ulch people began to make spears, shafts, and staffs out of that tree; they were hard and supple—you couldn't find any that were better!

Monokto went to get his flint. On the spot where Bolda's house and storehouses had stood there was now a swamp, and on the swamp blue lights were flitting from his old father's flint, guarding the cursed spot.

The people bowed to Monokto; now they remembered his name.

"Thank you, Monokto," they said, "for ridding us of Bolda!"

The Hare and the Magpie

There once lived a hare. He was a hare like any other hare, only—who knows why—he liked to boast before the others about what he was not: that he was strong, that he was brave, that he was a good hunter . . .

One day the hare found the carcass of a wild goat in a field.

No sooner had he sat down to eat it than a magpie came flying by.

She saw what a catch the hare had, sat down on a branch, said hello, and then asked, "Say, neighbor, where did you get such a big carcass?"

"I killed it," said the hare.

The magpie was amazed—a hare killing a wild goat!

The braggart wouldn't stop. "I'm such a good hunter that if I had really gone hunting, I would have killed all the animals around a long time ago! I can kill as many animals as I want! After I finish eating the goat, I'll go kill a bear."

The magpie bowed to the hare. "Say, neighbor, teach me to hunt like you. I am always hungry."

"Why not!" answered the hare. "It's very simple to hunt that way. All you have to do is open your mouth wide and yell. It's very simple. Don't you know how to yell?"

"Of course I know how! I know how to yell very well," said the magpie and thought to herself, "Why should I go looking for a bear when a hare is right under my nose?"

The magpie flew up higher, opened her mouth wide, and yelled. She yelled so loud that the titmice, sitting on nearby branches, fell to the ground.

The hare was frightened to death and dashed off. Where he ran, nobody knows.

The magpie sat a while, thought a while. "How is it that the hare ran off instead of falling down? I guess I didn't yell loud enough. Well, the next time I see a catch, I'll yell louder."

The magpie decided to fly all over the forest. As soon as she sees an animal, she starts yelling and chattering with all her might.

She herself has not killed a single animal with her shrieking. But hunters have noticed that a magpie yells when an animal is near. As soon as she begins to chatter and yell in the forest, the hunter rushes to where she is. The magpie tries her hardest—she chatters, opens her mouth wide, spreads her wings, shakes her tail wildly, and thinks, "Now I will kill him! Any moment now!" The hunter then appears, shoots the animal, and carries him off.

But sometimes it also happens that the magpie sees a hunter waiting in ambush. She is so glad: "Oh, how big he is! Now I will get him!" And she yells so loud she scares all the animals off, so there is nothing either for her or for the hunter.

The Birch Boy

It is a great misfortune when a man is lazy and envious.

An old man lived in an Oroch village. He had a son named Ulenda. Ulenda's appearance was good in every way: he was well-spoken, broad-shouldered, strong, and handsome. The young man was a beautiful sight! The only trouble was that Ulenda didn't like to work. He never wanted to do anything.

When he went hunting in the taiga he would lie down and go to sleep as soon as he saw mossy ground. When his father sent Ulenda fishing, he would sit down on the riverbank, look at the water, and spend the whole day just sitting and doing nothing. When his father sent him to look after the reindeer herd, Ulenda would sit down on a tree stump, throw back his head, and count clouds in the sky—and all the reindeer would wander off.

And that is why, even in his old age, the father had to provide for both himself and his son.

The old man was annoyed. All the other sons fed and took care of their fathers; only Ulenda still sat on the old man's back.

The old man went to the zangin—the judge—and said, "Help me, wise zangin! I can't feed a grown son any longer. I don't have the strength! Tell me, what should I do?"

The zangin thought and thought—he thought for a long time; he smoked up one hundred pipes while he thought.

Finally he said, "A lazy son is worse than a stone around your neck. A bow with a damp bowstring will not shoot. You have to change the bowstring. You need another son."

The old man groaned. "I am old! Where am I going to get another son?"

The zangin told him, "Tomorrow, go to the taiga. There you will see an ironwood birch tree standing between two elms. Chop the birch tree down. On it you will find your younger son, rocking in a little cradle. Bring him up, and you will have a helper!"

The old man went into the taiga. He walked and walked, until he saw an ironwood birch tree standing between two elms.

The old man started to chop down the birch tree. He struck it once, he struck it twice. He had broken his ax, but there wasn't even a notch on the tree. That was some birch tree! The old man grew tired. He lay down to rest and fell sound asleep.

And he had a dream that a bear came up to him and said, "To the right, in a hollow, there are two rivers. In one the water is white and in the other, red. Take some of the red water in your bowl and sprinkle it on the birch tree!"

The old man awoke. He stood up and went to look for the two rivers. Making his way through the dry branches in the forest, he tore all his clothes to tatters—his robe, his tunic, his trousers, his boots.

He climbed down into the hollow, and there he saw the two rivers.

He dipped some of the red water into his bowl and walked back.

He went to the birch tree and sprinkled it with the red water.

Then the old man again started to chop down the birch tree. He gave it only one blow—the tree swayed and fell to the ground.

The old man saw a cradle hanging in the fork of the trunk. In the cradle lay a child—a boy, no bigger than a bone needle. His face was round like the moon; his eyes were black, shining like two beads.

The old man said to himself, "Oy-ya-kha! I'll have to wait a long time for my adopted son to grow up and feed me!"

But the birch boy answered him, "When starting out on a journey, father, don't count the steps!"

The old man slung the cradle with the child over his shoulder and started for home.

He walked and walked. But what was this? With each step the cradle became heavier and heavier. By the time the old man had reached the village, the cradle had bent his shoulders down with its weight. The old man lowered the cradle to the ground—he had no more strength to carry it! But he looked and saw that the cradle had become huge. And the birch boy had grown very big. He climbed out of the cradle, bowed to the old man, and said, "Thank you, father, for setting me on my feet."

Then they walked on, side by side.

The old man called his younger son Kalduka.

They began to live together—the old man, Ulenda, and Kalduka.

Before the old man could turn around, Kalduka was grown and had caught up with Ulenda. He worked hard enough for three. He was strong and clever.

Whenever he fought anyone with sticks, his opponent's hands would be empty almost before he could blink. The reindeer herd doubled under his care. There was more than enough dried fish in the house. And there were plenty of furs—for themselves and for sale.

But Ulenda remained the same. The more he lay on his back, the lazier he became. He lay on his bunk, and his laziness grew greater and greater—it could scarcely fit inside the house any more.

The old man kept two eagles: one with a red beak, the other with a black one. Every autumn he plucked their tail feathers. He had been giving the red eagle's tail feathers to Ulenda, but now that he had such a hard-working new son, the old man gave the red eagle's tail feathers to Kalduka instead. He said, "Kalduka feeds me, so he is the older."

Ulenda said nothing. He endured the insult, but he was furious with his younger brother. He started to think how he might pay the birch boy back, how he might hurt him. He even forgot his laziness. His fury turned out to be stronger than his laziness.

Ulenda started to steal game from Kalduka's traps. He started to steal fish from Kalduka's nets.

Kalduka went to the zangin. "Wise man, find the thief!"

The zangin answered Kalduka, "Can anyone find a thief among his own?"

The zangin made a fire. He held a cat over the fire. The cat began to screech, and its face became contorted.

The zangin then said, "Let it be as the law wills. Let the thief's face become crooked, like this cat's. Then you will find the thief yourself."

Kalduka went home. Ulenda was hiding in a corner with a cloth wrapped around his face. Kalduka asked, "What's the matter with you, brother?"

"Nothing," answered Ulenda. "I've got a toothache."

Then a wind blew up and tore the cloth off Ulenda's face. Everybody saw that his face was crooked. Everybody saw that he was the thief. From that time on they called him Ulenda Crooked-Face.

Ulenda began to hate his birch brother more than ever. Day and night he tried to figure out how to ruin Kalduka, how to destroy him. But as long as the old man was alive, Ulenda could do nothing.

Time passed. The old man got sick and died. They had a funeral, and they cried over him. The zangin broke a spear over the old man and threw the pieces in different directions, so that the hunter's soul would depart from his body. They buried the old man.

One day Ulenda said to Kalduka, "Let us go to the island. We'll pick some day lilies and eat their sweet roots."

They rowed a boat to the island. When they arrived, the younger brother went to pick day lilies. He went into the taiga far from the shore. Ulenda jumped into the boat and rowed away, abandoning his brother on the island.

"Let the bird Kori eat him up!"

In those days the bird Kori lived on Khekhtsir Mountain. She was as

big as a storm cloud. When the bird Kori flew out of her nest, she covered the sky, so that everywhere it became completely dark. Woe to those who got in her way! They were never found again.

Kalduka walked all around the island, then came back to the shore. He saw that Ulenda was not there. Kalduka shouted and shouted. He called his brother again and again, but there was no answer. Kalduka ate some sweet day-lily roots and lay down on the ground. He lay there for a while, got nice and warm, and fell asleep.

The sun set. The bird Kori flew up from behind Khekhtsir Mountain. She covered the whole sky, and it became completely dark. As she flew, her wings sounded like a hard rain. The air whistled as though a strong wind were blowing.

Kalduka awoke. He became frightened and grabbed his bow.

The bird Kori was already over him. She was snapping her beak, and her eyes burned like two campfires.

Kalduka shot an arrow. But it was of no use—the bird's feathers were made of iron. Kori seized Kalduka in her talons and said, "Riddle me three riddles. If I can guess them, it's death to you. If I can't, I'll take you back to your home!"

Kalduka thought a while and agreed. Then he asked this riddle. "What is this: a frog is sitting on a rock and cannot jump off."

Kori thought and thought, but couldn't guess.

Kalduka said, "It's the nose on a face."

Kalduka asked the second riddle. "What is this: it came out of a place, went to another place, but how it got there it would not tell."

Again Kori couldn't guess it.

"It is an arrow," Kalduka told her.

And he asked the bird Kori a third riddle. "What is this: one hundred young men sleep on one pillow without quarreling."

The bird Kori couldn't guess this riddle either.

"It is poles on a roof," Kalduka said.

Then the bird seized Kalduka, lifted him into the air, and flew off. Whether she flew a long time, I do not know. She put Kalduka down near his home. Kalduka entered the house. When Ulenda saw him, he became pale with fear, began to quake, and said, "The wind carried me from the island. There was such a storm that I couldn't row."

Kalduka said nothing.

They went on living together. Kalduka hunted and fished, and Ulenda Crooked-Face lay on his back. But his anger didn't subside. He thought and thought, and one day he said to Kalduka, "I miss our father. I have heard that if you smear a dead man's lips with the saliva of the serpent Simu, it will bring him back to life. It would be so good to bring our father back to life!"

"And where is that serpent?" Kalduka asked. "How do you find her?"

"In the headwaters of the River Khor," said Ulenda.

Kalduka saddled a reindeer, mounted it, and rode off. Whether he rode for a long time, who knows? While he was gone, mushrooms grew thirty times on a fallen elm. Kalduka came to the river. He dismounted. He slapped the reindeer on the neck, turned it into a tree, and left it on the riverbank. Then he continued on foot. He came to a village. He saw that the Oroches lived there and that they were very sad. Kalduka asked them why they were so sad. They answered that the serpent Simu had been crawling into their village, eating people, and burning yurts—that there was no deliverance from her.

"How is that?" asked Kalduka. "Can't any of you kill the serpent?"

"We tried," the Oroches answered him. "But when the serpent breathes fire, people's hands wither. And you can't do anything without hands."

Kalduka thought a while and said, "I'll try. Maybe mine won't wither!"

He sharpened his spear, whetted his knife, picked up an iron pot in the village, and went into the forest where the serpent Simu lived. He wrapped himself in moss. He collected some wood pitch and put it into the pot. He dipped himself in the river and got all wet. Then he began to beat the pot with his spear; he made a lot of noise.

Simu heard the noise and crawled out of her hole. As she crawled and hissed, she left a red track—grass and stones were on fire behind her.

The serpent saw Kalduka and breathed her fire on him.

The wet moss shielded Kalduka from the fire. He swung his arm with all his might and threw the iron pot filled with pitch into the serpent's mouth. The pitch melted, and it plugged up Simu's throat. The serpent writhed, shuddered, and stretched out dead. White foam bubbled out of her mouth instead of fire. Kalduka gathered up the foam and started back.

Suddenly he heard the trees crackling. The taiga was smoking, the animals were running out of it, and the birds were flying away in flocks.

The Oroches said to Kalduka, "Woe to us, son! You killed Simu, but now her brother Khimu is coming to avenge his sister. Woe to us!"

"No!" said Kalduka. "Woe is only to those who have no heads on their shoulders."

He took seven iron pots, piled one on top of the other, and crawled under the bottom one.

Then Khimu swooped down. Everything was shaking. The earth was trembling, pieces were flying out of the sky. Khimu saw the pots, flung himself at them, and hit them hard! He broke through six iron pots with his head, but the seventh was too much for him—he cracked his head on it. Khimu hissed and crawled into the taiga—to die. Then Kalduka climbed out from under the pots. The Oroches surrounded him. They were happy that they had met such a bogatyr, that they were rid of the serpent Simu. They invited him into their clan; they wanted to adopt him as their son. The Oroch girls cast glances at him—any one of them would have been happy to marry a young man like that!

The old men said to him, "Stay with us."

"No, I must go home," Kalduka said.

But he had taken a fancy to one of the girls in the village. They went walking until they came to the riverbank. There they sat down on a tree.

Kalduka said, "Be my wife, girl! Come with me!"

Kalduka slapped the tree, and the tree turned into a reindeer. The reindeer flew with them back to Kalduka's village.

At home Ulenda was singing; he thought Kalduka was lost for good.

But Kalduka—suddenly there he was, and with a young wife!

Ulenda Crooked-Face grew more furious than ever with his brother. He thought to himself, "I will die, or I will destroy Kalduka and take his wife for myself!"

Kalduka went to the zangin and told him everything. He said that he had gotten the saliva of the serpent Simu to bring their father back to life, as Ulenda Crooked-Face had wanted.

The zangin smoked a pipe of tobacco, then said to him, "You are a birch boy, you do not know that people are not born twice. Why disturb the old man? And Ulenda sent you not for that, but for death!"

The zangin took the serpent's saliva and threw it in the river. The river began to seethe and to hiss. Steam rose from the water. Fish floated to the surface with their bellies up, dead.

"You see!" said the zangin. "Ulenda Crooked-Face would have killed you with this saliva."

Then the zangin sent for Ulenda Crooked-Face.

"Go into the taiga, Ulenda," he said. "You don't like people. You don't belong with them. Go into the taiga. There the taiga people live separately, each by himself. Be what you are in your soul."

So Ulenda went into the taiga. As he walked, fur grew on his body, and claws appeared on his hands and feet. At first Ulenda walked on two feet, then he dropped down and ran on all fours. Ulenda Crooked-Face became a bear.

And Kalduka started to live with his wife. They lived well. They had many children, and Kalduka was lucky in everything he did.

All this happened a long time ago—so many years ago that if you counted them on your fingers, there would not be enough fingers among all the old men in the village. You would have to borrow some from the children. But the children are running around—you can't catch them. So try and find out when this was!

Sable Souls

In the old days the Udege were numerous. Their villages were so close that the children could throw a stone from one to the next. The Udege lived along the seashore from the Koppi River to the Khadi Gulf and along all the mountain rivers in the Sikhote Alin Mountains. The smoke from their hearths rose to the sky like a storm cloud. When white swans flew over the villages, they turned black from the smoke.

In those times two brothers—Kanda and Yegda—lived on the Khungari River. Their father was an ordinary person. But the brothers—I don't know whom they took after—grew up to be what people don't become any more. They were as tall as a larch with seventy annual rings. They were so strong that wherever they stepped deep holes remained in the ground. When Kanda and Yegda traveled on skis, they overtook the migrating birds. Among all their kinsmen there were no hunters such as Kanda and Yegda. They didn't consider bears a catch—they could strangle them with their bare hands. They could catch a tiger on the run. They could grab a leopard by the tail.

Most of all, the brothers liked to hunt sable.

The sable is a cunning animal. It gives the hunter a long chase. A hunter has no time to eat or drink when he's chasing sable. The sable goes round and round in circles and muddies its tracks. Then it climbs into the hollow of a tree. Try and smoke it out of there!

But Kanda and Yegda didn't have to spend much time chasing a sable. The sable could run fast, but the brothers could run faster! When they tired the sable out, it would run into the forest and jump into the hollow of a tree. Then Kanda would stand at the hollow, while Yegda pushed the tree with one hand. The tree would start swaying, and the sable would come jumping out of the hollow. Kanda would hold his hat at the ready. How could the sable get away?

And that was how the brothers hunted.

They caught all the sables in their uncle's allotted plot. Then they began hunting sable elsewhere. They began hunting in other people's plots. And the other people were offended.

They said to the brothers, "You are taking our catch. You are taking our animals—this means you look upon us as dead. It's just as if you had killed us. This is how we look at it. To us this is a blood matter. We will take you to court—why have you killed us?"

But Kanda and Yegda only laughed. They were showing off their strength. They were not afraid of blood vengeance. They were not afraid of the court. They were not afraid of the zangin, the judge.

"A big animal for a big hunter!" they said.

"What kind of animal do you need?" asked the zangin. "You've been taking other people's animals. You have to pay a fine."

"We won't pay a fine, and we won't stop hunting sable," the brothers answered. "We'll keep hunting sable until we catch the Master of Sables!"

The zangin saw that Kanda and Yegda didn't believe in law and wouldn't listen to anyone; he became angry. He broke his staff in half and threw the pieces in different directions: the grievance against the brothers still stood.

The brothers went sable hunting. They wanted to catch the Master of Sables. They had heard from the old men that there was such a sable: three times as big as other sables, black as coal, fast as the wind; if you looked at him for a long time, you would go blind.

They searched over the whole taiga, but they couldn't find that sable.

While they looked for the Master of Sables, they killed all the other sables in the taiga. If they had at least made some use of their catch! But they would catch a sable, look at it, see that it was not the Master, and throw it away, having first torn it to pieces so that no one else could use it.

There was no life for the other hunters. There was no catch.

After a while Kanda and Yegda saw that they couldn't catch the Master of Sables by their own wits. The brothers went to the zangin. They bowed to him. "Would you know where the Master of Sables lives?"

"I am only a man," answered the zangin. "What do I know? Ask Onku—the Master of Mountains and Forests. He knows!"

"And where does Onku live?" the brothers asked.

"He lives on the highest peak of the Sikhote Alin Mountains, among the rocks and crags. His house is of stone. The road to his house is hard. And you can see him only if he wants you to."

"All right," said Kanda. "Let's go, brother!"

So they went.

At first they walked through the plain. They came to a red river. There they built a boat of birch bark. They crossed the river and walked through a birch forest. They came out to a yellow river. There they built a boat of poplar. They crossed the yellow river. They walked through a pine forest. Along the way they came to a white river. The river was seething and bubbling, like water boiling in a caldron, but the water in the river was cold; if you put your finger in it, your finger would be covered with a crust of ice. The brothers threw some big rocks into the river and crossed it by walking on the rocks.

On the other shore there was a cedar forest. The brothers heard three ravens and three owls screeching. Kanda and Yegda made their way through the cedars. The forest was as dense as a wall. The branches were tightly intertwined. The brothers started to fell the cedars to make a road. But behind them the felled trees sent roots into the ground again, and the trees stood back up to their full height.

A road had been there, but it had disappeared; only impenetrable forest was there now.

The brothers came at last to a high mountain. It was so high that if you looked at the top, your hat would fall off your head. The mountain had three levels. The brothers started to climb the mountain. Now six ravens and six owls screeched. Kanda decided that they were not too far from the Master's house now, and he started to call out. He called in such a loud voice that his shouts made the bark peel off the trees. But no one answered him. The brothers climbed on.

The forest came to an end. Now they were going through shrubs, but there were fewer shrubs than rocks. The farther they went, the more rocks there were. They walked among the crags. They climbed to the first level and rested. They started to climb to the second. The rocks slipped out from under their feet as though someone were pushing them. But Kanda and Yegda kept climbing higher. They got to the second level. They sat a while and rested. Then they started to climb to the third level. The crags stood in rows, they towered one upon another. The brothers looked and saw that the farther they went, the more the crags and rocks resembled people. They were alive. They had no eyes, but they watched the brothers—they turned as the brothers passed. Somehow Kanda and Yegda scrambled up to the third level. The stones kept slipping from under their feet and would not let the brothers touch them with their hands. Up above, nine ravens and nine owls were screeching.

Kanda said, "Well, brother, it looks as though we've finally come right to the Master's house!"

They climbed up on a crag. There they saw a stone house standing on ten posts. As tribal law required, it looked to the sunrise with two eyes—its windows. The house was so high that the roof was lost in the clouds. Inside, everything was as it should be: a bunk, a hearth, a place for bear, a place for old men. Only everything was so big that the brothers felt like little children there.

On the bunk sat something that looked like a big rock covered with moss.

Yegda shouted. He shouted so loud that the wind began to blow all around. "Hey, father, two people have come to see you! We have business with you!"

The moss-covered rock turned to the brothers. They looked and saw that it was not a rock—it was a man. Dark, as though made of stone, sinking into the earth to his waist from his own weight, he looked at the brothers with stony eyes.

His glance sent a chill through their hearts. It was Onku himself sitting before the brothers!

Kanda and Yegda bowed to him. They offered him elk meat and other human food. They said, "Father, help us to catch the Master of Sables! We told the zangin and our people that we would catch him! How can we go back on our word?"

Onku spoke, and the sound of his voice cracked the neighboring hills: avalanches tumbled from the mountains, the earth trembled.

"I have heard of you. There is a great complaint against you! Other people are offended: why have you destroyed all the sables? The Master of Sables is offended: there is nothing for him to do on the earth now. You won't catch him. When you killed the sables, their souls went to pasture in the heavens. The Master went with them."

The brothers started to think. They lighted their pipes. They gave one to the Master. As Onku drew on his pipe, smoke started coming out of the mountain tops, fire leaped up to the sky, and rocks flew upward. Clouds circled over the mountains, lightning flashed, and fiery rain began to pour down.

The brothers became very frightened and sat there more dead than alive. They thought some more. A bad thing had happened—they had wanted to show off their strength and daring, but it turned out that they had offended people. They had also offended the Master of Sables. And it appeared that Onku too was angry.

Kanda said, "Father, how can we bring the sables back to earth?"

The Master took his pipe out of his mouth, and the mountains stopped smoking. He said, "If a sable is killed in heaven, its soul comes down to earth and enters another sable."

Then Kanda said, "Well, brother, it looks as though you and I have to hunt sable in other places."

"It looks that way," answered Yegda.

They started to go back. But when they looked down they became dizzy—they had climbed so high to get to the Master! They didn't know how to get down. There were no roads to be seen, only sheer cliffs all around.

Then owls seized them and lifted them into the air. Suddenly everything vanished—the Master, the mountains, the rocks that looked like people. The brothers were standing near their native village.

The brothers started plaiting a rope. They used up a whole willow forest. They plaited such a long rope that if a good runner ran from sunrise to sunset, he could not run from one end of it to the other. They plaited a strong rope. Kanda tied one end of it to a red crag, the other to a black one. He struck the middle of the rope with his fist. The crags shattered into dust, but the rope remained intact.

Yegda threw one end of the rope into the sky. He caught the sky with a hook. Then the brothers pulled hard on the rope. They pulled the sky down toward the earth, and they tacked their end of the rope down with a small mountain. Then they took their hunting gear and some food, and they climbed the rope into the sky to hunt for sable souls.

They reached the sky.

At first they could see the earth below, then they went above the clouds.

The clouds were spread out below them like snow. There was a good, solid crust on top, as strong as a crust of ice. All around there were huge numbers of sable tracks! The hunters' hearts leaped. "What a sable hunt we'll have, brother!"

They hunted for a long, long time.

But no matter how many sables they killed, there were just as many left. The brothers started to get tired. Kanda said that he missed their home—that it would be nice to go home for a while.

The brothers went to look for the spot where they had climbed into the sky, but they couldn't find it.

While they had been hunting, spring had come on the earth. Young boars had begun to sharpen their tusks on the rope with which Kanda and Yegda had pulled the sky down to the earth. The boars had kept sharpening their tusks on it, and the rope had worn through. The sky had gone back up to its usual place.

The brothers walked and walked around the sky—they walked so long that their feet wore a road there, but they never came back down to earth. You can see that road very well at night—it stretches over the whole sky. Different people call it by different names, but the Udege say, "It is the Road of Heavenly People!" Yegda and Kanda keep walking on it—killing sables and sending their souls back to earth.

And since that time, sables haven't disappeared from the earth.

How the Fox and the Elk Exchanged Legs

One day a fox met an elk.

"What's new?" the fox asked the elk.

"Nothing's new, neighbor," the elk answered. "Yesterday I thought I was done for—a hunter was chasing me, and my antlers got entangled in the branches. My long legs are my misfortune. I'm so tall my antlers are always getting caught in the branches. And how are you doing?"

"Also badly, neighbor," said the fox. "The hunters lie in wait for me. My short legs are my misfortune. I stand too low to see anything around me!"

The animals grew sad because their lives were so hard and the world was so badly arranged. He who needed long legs had short ones, and he who needed short legs had long ones.

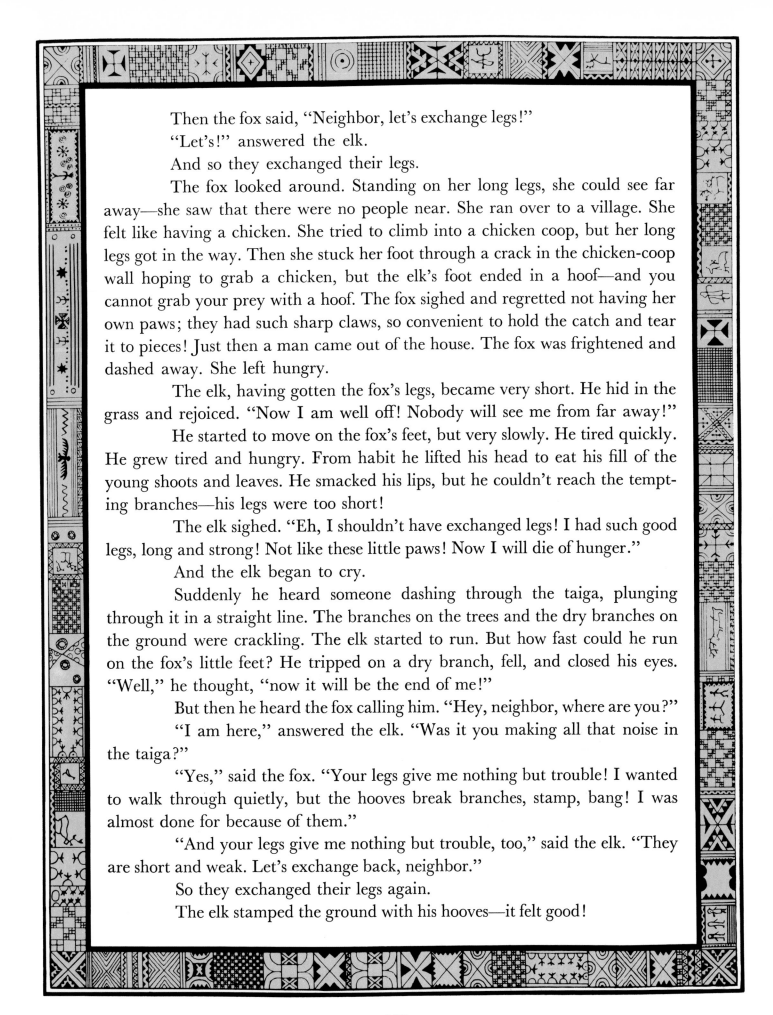

Then the fox said, "Neighbor, let's exchange legs!"

"Let's!" answered the elk.

And so they exchanged their legs.

The fox looked around. Standing on her long legs, she could see far away—she saw that there were no people near. She ran over to a village. She felt like having a chicken. She tried to climb into a chicken coop, but her long legs got in the way. Then she stuck her foot through a crack in the chicken-coop wall hoping to grab a chicken, but the elk's foot ended in a hoof—and you cannot grab your prey with a hoof. The fox sighed and regretted not having her own paws; they had such sharp claws, so convenient to hold the catch and tear it to pieces! Just then a man came out of the house. The fox was frightened and dashed away. She left hungry.

The elk, having gotten the fox's legs, became very short. He hid in the grass and rejoiced. "Now I am well off! Nobody will see me from far away!"

He started to move on the fox's feet, but very slowly. He tired quickly. He grew tired and hungry. From habit he lifted his head to eat his fill of the young shoots and leaves. He smacked his lips, but he couldn't reach the tempting branches—his legs were too short!

The elk sighed. "Eh, I shouldn't have exchanged legs! I had such good legs, long and strong! Not like these little paws! Now I will die of hunger."

And the elk began to cry.

Suddenly he heard someone dashing through the taiga, plunging through it in a straight line. The branches on the trees and the dry branches on the ground were crackling. The elk started to run. But how fast could he run on the fox's little feet? He tripped on a dry branch, fell, and closed his eyes. "Well," he thought, "now it will be the end of me!"

But then he heard the fox calling him. "Hey, neighbor, where are you?"

"I am here," answered the elk. "Was it you making all that noise in the taiga?"

"Yes," said the fox. "Your legs give me nothing but trouble! I wanted to walk through quietly, but the hooves break branches, stamp, bang! I was almost done for because of them."

"And your legs give me nothing but trouble, too," said the elk. "They are short and weak. Let's exchange back, neighbor."

So they exchanged their legs again.

The elk stamped the ground with his hooves—it felt good!

"It is well arranged," he said, "that the elk walks on hooves! His legs are strong, his hooves are solid!"

The fox took a run on her feet—it felt good! Her paws were light, her claws sharp, her gait silent.

The fox answered the elk, "Yes, that's right! It is well arranged that the fox has small feet with sharp claws."

They said good-bye and went off in different directions.

From that time on animals have not exchanged legs.

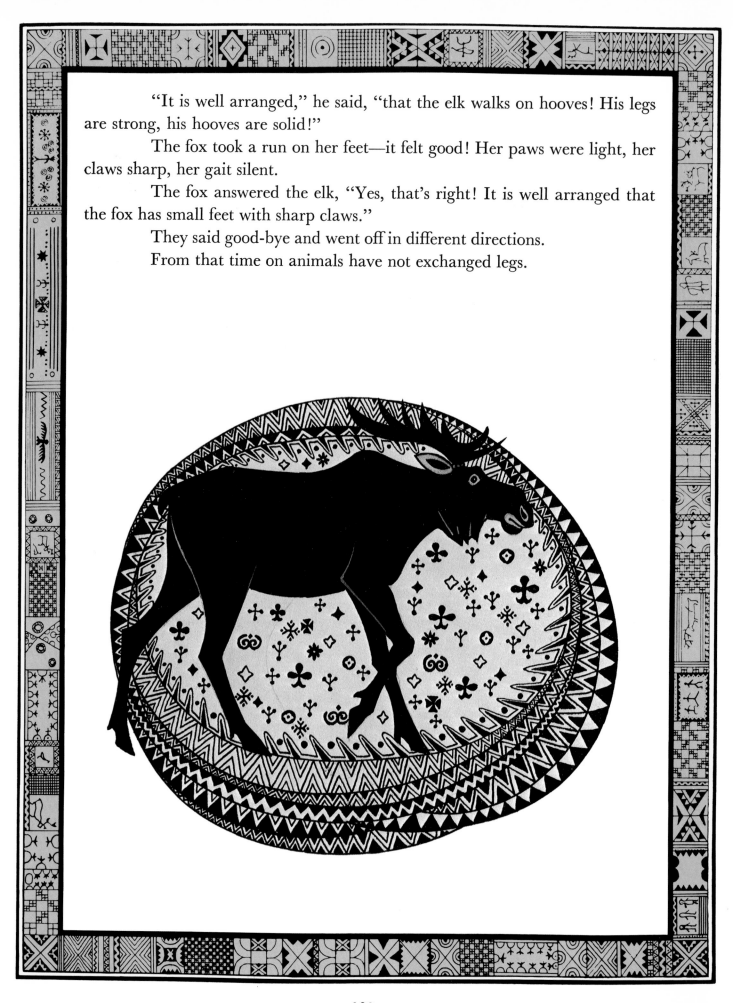

The Chinese Bride

If you are bad, do not expect good from others.

Solodo Khoinga, a Nivkh, lived on the Amur River. He was a rich man. He owned twenty dog teams. Ten angazas—poor men—netted fish for him in the river. Ten Manchurian bondsmen took care of his household for him, plaited ropes out of willows, and wove nets out of nettles. Ten Chinese bondswomen wove rugs for Solodo, sewed robes, cooked food, and picked berries. Ten storehouses held his goods.

Solodo was a greedy man. He had a lot of property, but he always wanted more. Greed is like a river: the farther it flows, the wider it becomes. Solodo walked around looking—what else could he take for himself? He moved his things from place to place, put them in order, admired them, and rejoiced.

Solodo had a son—Alumka. He wasn't exactly a good-looking young man: all his good looks were in his father's riches. He wasn't exactly a clever young man: all his cleverness was in his father's goods. But Solodo kept saying, "Never mind that Alumka is lacking something; my storehouses are full—he'll get by somehow!"

The time came for Alumka to marry.

His mother braided a band of dog hair and nettles to put on his bride's arm, and they started looking for a bride for Alumka. They prepared a good bride price. Alumka was proud of the high bride price and put on airs. None of the brides was good enough for him.

They showed him one bride.

"Her eyes are ugly," said Alumka.

People said to him, "Why are you hurting the girl's feelings? It's your own eyes that are crossed. That's why you can't see the bride properly."

Solodo waved his hand at the people. "My son is rich," he said. "He doesn't need looks. And it's good that his eyes look in different directions. With one eye he can look after the house and with the other at the river, to see if the angazas are doing their work properly."

About another bride Alumka said her hands were too small.

People said to him, "Why are you hurting the girl's feelings? Look at yourself: one of your hands is bigger than the other!"

Again Solodo stood up for his son. "It's not so bad that Alumka's hands are not the same size: he collects small money with his small hand and big money with his big one. No money will pass by Alumka's hands!"

Alumka did not like the third girl either.

"She is lame!" he said.

"Why are you hurting the girl's feelings? You are the one who is so bowlegged that a dog could run between your legs!"

Solodo patted his son on the shoulder. "What need has Alumka for straight legs? He doesn't have to go to the taiga—you will bring the animals to him. He doesn't have to go to the river—the hired men will catch the fish for him. My son has a master's legs: they are curved so they are more convenient for sitting and talking with the Chinese merchants."

Solodo and Alumka kept going around looking over the brides. They were shown another girl. Alumka snorted and pouted. "She is a fool!" he said.

People looked at Solodo and at Alumka. They didn't say anything, so as not to hurt the father's feelings.

They showed Alumka one more girl.

This time the young man's mouth watered.

The girl's skin was as white as the bark of a young birch. Her braid was down to her knees. Her hair was as black as night, soft and shiny. She had a beautiful face. She walked with her head tilted to the side, smiling. Her teeth were as white as the snow on sable hunting grounds.

Somehow Alumka managed to open his mouth. He said, "I'll have to think about it! Maybe I'll give my hand to this girl."

But this time Solodo frowned.

"What kind of a bride is she?" he said. "All they are giving for her dowry is bones. Only a rich bride will come into my house!"

No bride was found for Alumka among the Nivkhs.

He heard that people also live in the sky—merry people. They pour water onto the earth, they throw snow onto the earth. The sky women are beautiful and playful. Sometimes they lower fishing lines with golden hooks to the earth to catch ordinary people.

Alumka thought, "I won't take an ordinary bride. I'll take a sky woman for a wife!" He walked around the village looking up at the sky. He did not watch the ground under his feet and tripped, bruising himself all over.

One day there was a rainbow arching over the village.

Alumka rejoiced. "Oho!" he said. "They must have lowered a fishing line from the sky! I'll climb a tree! I'll grab the hook, I'll pull on it, and I'll pull a sky woman down from the sky to the earth."

Alumka quickly climbed a hundred-year-old pine—climbing a tree is easy with bowlegs. He got all the way to the top, where he sat astride the uppermost branch, trying to see where the golden hook was dangling. But his eyes were looking in different directions, so he saw one branch from two sides. He mistook the branch he was sitting on for the sky hook. He tugged at it with all his might! And the branch broke.

Alumka went flying down to the ground. He hit the ground so hard that he lost what little mind he still had, and sparks flashed before his eyes.

"Eh," he said. "I didn't hold onto the hook firmly enough!"

His father saw that Alumka would be finished altogether if he fell off another such hook, and he decided to go with his son to the Chinese kingdom for a bride. He had heard that Chinese brides came with big dowries.

The berry is sweeter beyond far-off hills!

Solodo got ready for the journey to San-Sing. He took the pelts of a hundred sables, a hundred otters, a hundred squirrels, a hundred weasels, a hundred red foxes, ten seals, and ten bears. No one in the Khoinga clan had ever paid such a price for a bride! The Nivkhs shook their heads.

And Solodo kept saying over and over again, "With this bride price we'll get the emperor's daughter for Alumka!"

Alumka rejoiced, and why not? No Nivkh had ever married an emperor's daughter!

The Khoingas set out to get a bride.

They sailed up the Amur River. They came to the spot where the blue waters of the Amur meet the yellow waters of the Sungari. They turned into the Sungari. They entered the Chinese kingdom.

They sailed for a long time. They saw many people. The Chinese people came out on the riverbank, looked at Solodo and his son, and pointed at them with their fingers, as though they were examining a marvel of nature. Alumka kept asking his father, "Will it be soon?"

"Only a flea jumps soon," was the father's reply. The son had worn Solodo out by the time they reached their destination.

There the Khoingas were met like honored guests. "What can we do for you?" they were asked. The headman himself came out to greet Solodo. He appointed an interpreter to serve the Nivkhs.

Solodo said to his son, "Do you see how they receive us? The rich have kinfolk everywhere."

Father and son stayed for several days. Alumka walked along the streets, gawking at everything. The houses were tall—the roofs reached almost to the sky. On the roofs were stone dragons with their mouths open and their red tongues stuck out. The streets were filled with people. It was as noisy as a seal rookery. People were selling, people were buying, people were bartering.

The headman offered Solodo sea worms, nightingale tongues, swallow

nests, meat that melted in your mouth, cookies that must have been baked in heaven. Solodo ate everything. He choked with greed: you have to eat as much as you can, as long as they are giving it to you.

The headman said to him, "We will show you our very best brides!"

"Yes, yes!" Solodo answered. "Give us the very best! For such a bride price we must have the emperor's daughter! That's why we came!"

The headman took them to a large house to show them the brides. In the house there was a large room. In the room there were one hundred windows. In each window there were one hundred many-colored pieces of glass. Inside the room the brides stood in a row—so many of them that Solodo's eyes were dazzled. And Alumka saw twice as many: he saw each bride separately with each eye. Behind each bride stood a slave, and beside each slave the dowry was piled up like a mountain.

Solodo looked at the slaves; he wanted to pick a strong one. But Alumka stared at the brides. How could anyone decide which was the best? They all had their faces covered with veils.

Alumka said to the headman, "I'd like to see the face of one of them, at least!"

The headman answered, "You mustn't look at the emperor's daughters—you might go blind!"

"They are all good!" Solodo whispered to his son, trembling with greed. "Look at those dowries!"

The Nivkhs had come to the end of the row. Suddenly they looked and saw that there were two slaves behind one of the brides. Solodo almost jumped with joy. He hissed in his son's ear, "Choose this one! She must be the most imperial of all the emperor's daughters!"

The Khoingas paid the bride price and received their bride. With the bride the headman gave them a two-masted longboat, piled with silks, tea, rice, flour—enough for a whole year. Slaves carried the bride in their arms. "Our mistress," they said, "doesn't walk. Her feet are so tiny they cannot hold her up!"

Solodo couldn't take his eyes off the bride's clothing. Her robe was embroidered with gold dragons; on her head was a hat with little bells, birds, and flowers—you couldn't make out where the head began under it. On her arms silver bands were tinkling. In her hand was a fan of bamboo sticks and rice paper, decorated with gold. When Alumka's bride opened it, she was completely hidden behind it! Alumka wanted to look at the face of his betrothed, but the bride wouldn't let him take off her veil.

Solodo consoled him. "Be patient, Alumka, till we get home!"

The Khoingas started for home.

They were sailing on the Sungari River and were already approaching the Amur when suddenly pirates fell upon them. The pirates' beards were dyed red. Their spears were twice as long as a man's height. Their swords were two palms wide. They swooped down on the longboat in their black sampan with forty oars, like ravens on carrion!

The pirates robbed Solodo of everything—he barely managed to convince them to spare their lives. The pirates cleaned out the whole longboat. Alumka's bride sat in her rich clothing, not stirring. The pirates came up to her, surrounded her, raised her veil—and ran away in all directions! In one moment, they got off the longboat onto their black sampan with yellow sails and sailed off!

"They must have been nearly blinded by the beauty of the emperor's daughter," Solodo said to his son.

It takes less time to sail downstream than to tell about it. Solodo and his son sailed fast. They were happy that at least the pirates didn't take the bride, didn't dare to touch her.

They returned to their native village.

Even though they did not bring home the dowry, they brought a Chinese beauty into Alumka's house. Guests came running to the house to look at Alumka's bride. Alumka lifted her veil. The Nivkhs looked and ran off as fast as they could. Last out of the house was Solodo, crawling on all fours.

Alumka was astounded. Why did the Nivkhs all run away? He started to examine his wife. He examined her for three days.

He managed to cover one of his eyes with his hand, so it wouldn't get in the way. He looked—his wife was old enough to be his grandmother!

Alumka came out of the house. He sat a while; he smoked a while. He heard the whole village laughing at him. "He took an emperor's daughter for a wife!"

The Chinese woman shouted to him, "Where have you gone, my husband?"

"I'm going for a walk!" said Alumka. "Your beauty has hurt my eyes."

Alumka got into a boat and rowed away.

Where he went, who knows! Solodo sent twenty dog teams in different directions to look for his son. They never found him.

How a Bear Kept Reindeer

Once a herd of reindeer was grazing in a meadow. A tiger attacked the herd. He separated several reindeer from the herd and drove them into the taiga. One he tore to pieces, and the others ran away in fear. But they couldn't find the road back to the herd, so they began to pasture by themselves.

A bear met this group of reindeer.

The bear was old and could no longer hunt well; how much he had to eat I do not know, but his sides were sunken in, and his fur had become patchy and rumpled.

The bear saw the reindeer and thought to himself, "What luck has come my way! I will keep the reindeer. I will become a reindeer keeper like a man. The reindeer will have offspring, and I'll have enough meat for the rest of my life. And herding reindeer doesn't take much brains!"

The bear was happy. He drove the reindeer to a pasture close to his lair. He sat down nearby, pleased, looking at the reindeer and thinking about which one to slaughter first.

The reindeer saw that the bear wasn't bothering them, and they started to graze. They began looking for moss, walking with their heads bent to the ground. The bear watched them but didn't understand. What were the reindeer doing? It looked to him as if they were listening for something. The bear became frightened: maybe the reindeer were listening to see if their master was coming.

The bear went up to one of the reindeer and asked, "What are you listening for?"

The reindeer looked at him but didn't answer. The bear asked another one; that reindeer also looked at the bear but didn't answer either. The reindeer thought it was funny that a bear had decided to be a reindeer keeper, yet didn't know what reindeer ate!

The bear ran from one reindeer to another until he was out of breath. He said to himself, "This tending reindeer is hard work!"

As long as they could find moss, the reindeer grazed near the bear's lair; when they ate it all up, they started wandering away. Again the bear became frightened. If the reindeer continued this way, they would leave altogether. The bear didn't know that men move from place to place following their reindeer, and he started to drive his reindeer back. But while he was driving one back toward his lair, another would run away to look for moss and would disappear from sight.

The bear became completely exhausted, but he couldn't turn the reindeer back. He had to follow them. He walked after them, continually looking back—he was so sorry to leave his warm lair, his comfortable old lair! But he didn't want to lose the reindeer either. He sighed and continued walking, farther and farther from his lair.

"Oh," he said, "it's hard work herding reindeer! If I had known, I would never have taken it on!"

The bear traveled far from his lair.

Then he met a wolf and a fox.

"Hello!" they said. "What are you doing here?"

"You see," said the bear, "I've become a reindeer keeper."

The fox began to wag her tail and nod her head.

"It's about time," she said. "Neighbor wolf and I provided ourselves with reindeer a long time ago. Now we do well. We eat reindeer meat often."

"But the reindeer have really worn me out," said the bear.

"That's because you aren't used to the work," answered the fox. "You poor, poor neighbor! When you aren't used to it, it is very hard. I don't know how you are going to herd your reindeer during the winter."

The bear began to think: that's true—how would he manage with the reindeer during the winter? In the winter he would want to sleep, to hibernate, but if he fell asleep, the reindeer would wander off. Where, then, would he look for them when he awoke in the spring?

He said to the fox and the wolf, "Help me take care of my reindeer!"

The fox was crafty. For appearance' sake she looked thoughtful, but she had only one thing in mind—how to put something over on the bear. She said to him, "Oh, I don't know what we can do for you—we wouldn't be able to manage. It is very hard work. But we have to help one another. Give us your reindeer; when you come in the spring, we'll give them back."

And the fox and the wolf drove the reindeer into the taiga.

The bear started to dance—he was so happy! He said to himself, "I've tricked these fools! They'll be chasing after the deer all winter. And in the spring and summer I'll eat my fill—I'll get all the meat I want." The bear ran to his lair and curled up to sleep for the winter.

The fox and the wolf drove the herd farther into the forest. There the wolf slaughtered all the reindeer. The two cheats had plenty to eat all through the winter.

Meanwhile, the bear lay in his lair, sucking his paw. He was dreaming of reindeer: they were walking around so fat that the fat was dripping from them onto the ground. "Oh, will I have meat in the spring!" dreamed the bear. The more his stomach rumbled from hunger, the fatter the reindeer became in his dreams.

Spring arrived. The sun melted the snow. Streams ran along the ground. Buds appeared on the trees. The bear awoke from his long sleep and climbed out of his lair. He walked through the taiga, staggering from weakness. His sides were sunken in, and his fur was as patchy and rumpled as though he had some kind of a disease.

The bear searched out the fox and the wolf. They had eaten well through the winter and had become fat and sleek. The fox ran out to greet him; she bustled about as though she were so overjoyed she didn't know where to seat her dear friend. She spoke without stopping, not letting the bear open his mouth.

Finally the bear asked her, "Well, neighbor, where are my reindeer?"

The fox began to wail and to wave her paws. "A misfortune befell your reindeer, neighbor—the whole herd is lost!"

"What do you mean?" asked the bear, opening his mouth wide. "How did they get lost?"

"They ran away," answered the fox.

"What do you mean?" the bear again asked, getting angry. "How did they run away?"

"They just ran away, that's all! If you yourself, their owner, couldn't manage them, certainly we couldn't keep them!"

"And where are your own reindeer?" asked the bear as he looked around. He saw reindeer skulls and bones scattered everywhere.

The fox began to wail even more; she shed a tear and gave the wolf such a hard shove in the ribs that he also began to howl, from pain.

"Misfortune befell our herd too!" the fox cried at the top of her voice. "We couldn't preserve our herd either! The moths ate our reindeer, neighbor!"

"What do you mean?" asked the bear. "How?"

"This is how: the moths descended on the reindeer—their fur is so thick—and went to work eating them all up; we didn't have time to blink before all our property disappeared." The fox looked at the reindeer bones and howled at the top of her voice. "Ah, my dear ones! You were such good reindeer! I loved you so much, my darlings!"

The bear felt sorry for the fox. He began to comfort her. "Don't cry, neighbor, worse things can happen!" He scratched the back of his neck and thought a while. "There's nothing we can do if the moths ate them. It looks as if I'm not really made to be a reindeer keeper. I'll never keep reindeer again!"

And the bear trudged off into the taiga.

Since that time, bears have not gone near reindeer!

Discontented Lado

All this happened a very long time ago. So much time has passed since then that where a river once flowed, mountains now stand; where rocks once lay, forests have grown.

⊛

A daughter was born in the house of the hunter Chumdaga of the Dungu clan.

Chumdaga had waited for a child for a long time. He had very much wanted to have a son, but he was glad of a daughter too. And the mother simply didn't know what to do with herself for joy.

They gave their daughter a good name—Lado.

The old folks did everything they could to have their daughter grow up good, beautiful, and happy. The mother didn't call her daughter by name for a whole year, so the evil demons wouldn't find out about her birth—she called her "my pretty," "my dear." The mother hung a bear's tooth over her daughter's cradle to scare away the evil demons. She also hung over it a bird made of tinder wood, birchbark earrings, and a rooster's claw so the daughter wouldn't cry, and a hunchbacked old woman carved of wood so the daughter would have good dreams. The mother bathed the daughter in her own milk. She made her a pillow of eiderdown and a bed of the softest cuckoo feathers.

And Lado grew up to be a beauty of beauties.

Her face was round and white, like the full moon; her eyes were black, like currants; her cheeks were pink, like wild rosemary in the spring; her lips were like red raspberries. Lado grew up as shapely as the day-lily blossom. That's how beautiful she was!

The old folks gazed at their daughter and couldn't rejoice enough.

Only one thing turned out badly: Lado did not know how to do anything. The mother didn't want her daughter to have rough hands, so the daughter never made a fire, never chopped wood, never caught fish with a fish spear, never held an oar in her hands, and never worked pelts. The mother didn't want her daughter's eyes to get red from work, so the daughter never embroidered robes with silk, never sewed pelts, never had to choose reindeer hair for embroidery. It came down to Lado's not even knowing how to knead dough or bake cakes. Lado did not know how to do a single thing.

Lado walked around the village, shapely and graceful. The young men couldn't take their eyes off her. They looked at beautiful Lado and shook their heads in wonder, but they didn't dare approach her.

A young man came to court Lado. There was no hunter better than he in the whole village: when animals met him, they cried, knowing they could not get away from him. The young man came courting, but Lado pouted and turned her nose to the side. "Get away from me, you—you smell of animals! How could I ever live with you? I would hurt my hands, working your pelts."

Another young man came to court Lado. There was no fisherman better than he in the whole village: he could catch ten fish at once with one fish spear, and in winter he could see through the ice and find the hollows where the fish were hiding. The young man came courting, but Lado turned completely away from him and held her nose with her fingers. "Get away from me, you—you smell of fish! How could I ever live with you? I would always be wet."

A third young man came to court Lado. He had the best dog team in the village: his dogs were as fast as the wind. No one could compete with them. The young man came courting Lado, but she did not even look at him. As soon as the young man had appeared on the doorstep, Lado began to wave her hands and buried her nose in her eiderdown pillow. "Get away from me, you—you smell of dogs! How could I live with someone like you? I would wear out my feet, feeding your dogs."

The suitors all gave up on Lado. They said, "Why do you reproach us with our work? That isn't nice."

The mother heard them. She said to the daughter, "You are treating people badly. You shouldn't hurt their feelings."

Lado became angry with her mother, waved her hands, became red with fury, and began to yell. "I know you have wanted to marry me off and get rid of me for a long time!"

"What are you saying, daughter?" the mother asked. "Live whatever way you want to live. Live with us your whole life."

She calmed her daughter down, and Lado stopped yelling.

But who rolls down a mountain rolls the rocks down with him. Lado chased away all her suitors and then became displeased with her parents too. Lado pouted. Why is mother wearing an ugly robe? Why did father come home all wet from fishing? Nothing pleased her.

The mother served her some cereal.

"Why is it thick?" the daughter yelled.

The mother served her some fish.

"Why is it flabby?" Lado stamped her feet.

The mother served her some meat.

"Why is it tough?" the daughter yelled again.

The mother put some cakes on the table.

"Why are they bitter?" beautiful Lado spat out.

The mother began to cry. There was no way of pleasing her daughter! She called in the neighbor children and gave them the cakes.

The children ate the cakes and praised them. "Oh, mother, they are so tasty, so soft, so sweet!"

Then Lado became furious. She pushed her mother away, stamped her feet, yelled, and flew out of the house. She looked around her. Everything

looked bad to her—dirty and smoky, and all the people were ugly. She looked up and saw some swans flying overhead. Their feathers were shiny, like clean snow. The swans were flying who knows where, flying away from the winter.

Lado shouted, "I will roll over, I will cry, I will become a white swan! I will fly with the swans to unknown lands. I will look for clean people! I will find a new mother!"

She rolled over, and instantly she was covered with snow-white feathers; she rose into the air on swan wings and began to fly.

The mother began to weep and called out to her daughter. But selfish Lado didn't even look back at her mother.

Lado flew up to the flock of swans.

They asked her, "Where are you from, new sister?"

Lado answered, "I will fly with you to look for clean people, who don't smell of fish! I will look for a new mother in unknown lands!"

But the swans did not make room for Lado; they did not admit her into the flock.

The leader flapped his wings and said, "How can you find a new mother? A human being has only one mother. There is no other!"

The swans would not accept Lado, so she flew by herself. On she flew, furious at her mother and furious at the swans. "I'll fly to a new place. I'll find a place where people don't smell of fish, where people don't smell of animals, where people don't smell of dogs. I'll find a clean place. I'll find a new mother for myself!"

The swans flew away. Lado flew away too.

The mother cried for a long time after losing her daughter.

The trees dropped their leaves. The hare put on a white coat. The snakes fell asleep among the rocks. The bear went to sleep in his lair. Hunters went off after sable. The Master of Waters covered the river with a roof of ice against the cold.

And the mother still cried, still looked in the direction in which Lado had flown away.

Once again all the roads became black. The bear stopped sucking his paw. The squirrels had eaten up all their nuts. The warbler came flying back from the lands beyond the sea.

But the mother still cried, still watched the sky, still looked in the direction in which Lado had flown away. The mother was so busy watching the sky all the time, she sometimes forgot about the fire in the hearth. The fire began to go out and then went out altogether. When the fire went out of the house, life went out of the house. Lado's mother died.

Then a warm wind blew from the Chinese kingdom. Through the old grass new grass began to send up shoots. The Master of Waters took the ice roof off the river. The bear came out of his lair. The hare lost his white coat in the forest. Buds appeared on the trees. Migrating birds came flying back to their old haunts.

The swans came flying back from far-off lands.

Lado too flew back. It looked as if she hadn't found a new mother for herself. She started to circle over her village. She started to fly over her house. She shouted, calling to her mother, "I will roll over, I will cry, I will become a girl again! I will embrace my old mother, I will dry her tears."

But no one came out of the house. No one answered. Lado hovered in the sky, weeping. She could not turn back into a girl.

All summer long Lado flew over her native village. She kept waiting for her mother to come out of the house to meet her. But no one came. And when the cold wind began to blow from the Amur River, Lado flew away to warmer lands.

Ever since then she comes flying back every spring, calling for her mother—but no one answers.

An Empty Head

A young man by the name of Chungu lived in the Zaksorov clan. He was a young man like any other young man: he had two ears, two eyes, one nose, two legs, two arms, and one head. Only it was said that Chungu's head was completely empty. Chungu worked little and ate much. Chungu thought little for himself and believed everything he heard. And that's how he lived. He ate, he slept, he sat on the riverbank, he scratched his head, and he went nowhere.

His father tried to teach him to hunt—he wanted to take him along into the taiga.

They dressed Chungu in full hunters' attire. They put elkskin boots with silk embroidery on him, embroidered kneeguards, trousers of the best leather, a white robe embroidered with reindeer hair, and a belt of ducks' heads. They put a silk-embroidered band on his head and a hat made of musk-deer pelts with a squirrel's tail. They put a carved spear in his hands. They hung a bow and arrows at his side, and two knives—one straight and one curved—on his belt.

Chungu became a handsome young man.

He liked his outfit. He stood slapping his robe with his hand. He laughed aloud with joy.

His father said to him, "That's enough, Chungu. Let's go."

Chungu shook his head. He did not want to leave the village and spoil his joy.

His father spoke to him again: "Beauty is not in a man's clothes but at the end of his spear! Let's go, son!"

But Chungu wasn't listening. He was rejoicing in himself. He started to dance. He stamped his feet in place, he circled, he slapped his robe and his trousers. He dropped his arrows, and his spear was poking in all directions—any minute it might maim someone.

Then the father became angry. He tapped his son on the head. Chungu's head clanked like a copper kettle. The father became frightened.

"Oy-ya-kha!" he cried. "My son's head must really be empty! That is bad! What should I do?"

He did not try to take his son hunting again. How much game can you catch with an empty head?

Chungu sat down on the riverbank. He found something to do—he gazed at himself in the water, admiring his clothes, and he kept tapping his empty head. He made so much noise that it could be heard through the whole village.

The Nanai came running from all over—they thought someone was playing on musical logs at an odd time. They looked and saw that it was Chungu, banging his empty head! So they laughed and went home.

And that's how things went on.

Chungu's father went hunting, and he fished in the Amur.

His mother salted the fish, worked the pelts, cooked the food, and fed her son and husband.

But Chungu wasn't good for anything. All he did was sit on the riverbank, scratching and banging his head.

I do not know how much time passed this way. The old folks got older and grew weaker. The mother started to get tired from her work—it was harder and harder for her to do everything alone.

She said to the old man, "I can't do all the work by myself any longer."

The father and mother sat and smoked a while, thought a while.

The father said, "We'll have to find a wife for Chungu. Then you will have a helper."

"How can we find a wife for Chungu?" the mother asked. "His head is empty. Who will give a daughter to him?"

"If we give a good bride price, someone will," the father answered.

The old man and the old woman started to put a bride price together.

They took a large copper kettle, a sword that came from beyond the seas, three silk robes and three fur robes, a copper mirror, twelve pairs of earrings, a spear trimmed with silver, three pieces of silk cloth, a tunic of bamboo armor with brass buckles from distant islands, a bowstring as long as a hunter is tall, and a warrior's bow trimmed with bone. They put together a rich bride price!

Still, no one in the village wanted to marry Chungu.

In a neighboring village lived an old woman with her daughter; the old woman was very poor. Her daughter's name was Anga. Except for one dog team, Anga had no dowry. The old woman and her daughter were so poor they didn't even have blankets.

Chungu's parents proposed marriage to Anga. Anga cried a while, but what could she do? She agreed. She thought that life would now become easier for her mother.

Anga knocked the ashes out of her pipe at her doorstep, so as not to carry fire away from her mother's home, so as not to carry happiness away from it. She stepped onto her own pot with one foot, then from her pot she stepped onto her bridegroom's pot, which had been placed outside the threshold, as tradition required. Then Chungu took Anga home.

They came to Chungu's house. The young man sat down on the bunk. He ate his fill of meat and began to boast, "Wife, do you know what kind of man I am? There is no man like me anywhere! Do you know what kind of head I have? No one has a head like mine!"

Chungu tapped on his head. The head hummed like a dry larch on a windy day.

Anga became frightened. "Oh, my husband's head is completely empty! How can I live with someone like that?" And Anga began to cry.

Chungu couldn't understand why his wife was crying. He sat and said nothing. Then he fell asleep.

Anga looked at him. He had a nice face, just like other people's: two eyes, two ears, one nose. Anga became angry. Why should a man with an empty head have a nice face like other people's? She decided: "Let your face not be a nice face, so that you won't fool people with your looks!"

She took some red clay from the hearth. She took some black soot from the hearth. She dissolved the clay and the soot. Now she had paint in two colors—black and red.

Anga painted Chungu's face with red and black designs. She painted it in such a terrible way she even became frightened herself.

Chungu slept for a long time; finally he awoke. He was thirsty. He picked up a birch-bark bowl of water and started to drink. From habit, he looked in the water, and he saw his reflection. Chungu did not recognize himself. He asked, "Hey, you, who are you? What are you doing in my bowl?"

He looked around—everything else was familiar: his hearth, his house, his wife sitting on the bunk. But the face was not his.

Chungu called, "Anga, come here! Someone got into my bowl—a strange kind of face."

Anga asked, "Who is calling me?"

"It is I calling you," said Chungu. "It is I, Chungu, your husband."

Anga shook her head. "How can you be Chungu? My husband has a nice face, but yours is a horrible fright!"

"That's true," said Chungu. "I have a good-looking face, I am a handsome man, I have seen that myself."

Chungu thought and thought, and said, "What a bad thing has happened! I must have lost my face somewhere. I'll go look for it."

Chungu got up from the bunk. He went out of the house. He walked along the road, looking down at his feet. He tapped his head—and it hummed. Chungu was happy.

"It is I!" he said. But then he looked in the river and became sad—he saw a strange face. "No," he said, "it is not I."

Chungu bumped into people as he walked. He asked everyone he met, "Have you, by any chance, seen Chungu?"

People laughed at him.

"No, we haven't," they said.

Chungu scratched his head.

"It looks as if he's not in this village," he said. "I'll go farther on."

So Chungu went to look for himself. He left the village and did not return. To this day he cannot find himself. And no one was sorry that he left.

Of what use is a lazy man or an empty-headed fool?

The Fleetest of Foot

Once the animals had an argument about who could run the fastest.

The wolf said, "I am the fastest! When I run, the bushes flash by my eyes and the wind whistles in my ears!"

The bear said, "No, I am the fastest! When I run, the trees crackle and the branches fly off in all directions!"

The fox listened to them and said, "I am the one who runs the fastest. When I run, my paws flash by so quickly that I can't even see them."

The hare looked at them all.

"What's the sense of your arguing?" he said. "I am the fastest of all! When I run, I see nothing, I hear nothing! That's how fast I run!"

They argued for a long time. Finally they decided to have a race. They would run to the next small hill and back. They lined up and started off. The hare ran up to the small hill, turned around, and ran back.

He came back quickly, sat down, and waited for his friends.

The wolf came back only toward evening. The fox came running back in the middle of the night. The bear came trudging back toward morning.

Then they met and decided: "The hare is the fastest of us all." And they all went home.

The hare started to do somersaults from joy. He did somersaults and sang, "Here I am, the fleetest of foot! Here I am, so fleet of foot, the fleetest of foot am I!"

A mouse saw him and became envious. She came up to the hare and said hello. Then she said, "They were wrong to call you the fleetest of foot!"

"What do you mean, wrong!" The hare was insulted. "We had a race, and I was the first to get back. I won over everyone else!"

"You should have waited for me."

"Well, let's you and me have a race," said the hare. "Let's run!"

"And how do you run?" asked the mouse.

"I run fast," the hare said. "When I run, I see nothing, I hear nothing! That's how fast!"

So they started to race. The mouse ran a short distance, then sat down under a hummock and hid. She completely disappeared from sight.

And the hare flew. He saw nothing, he heard nothing. He sped along. He ran to the small hill and then turned back. He ran with all his might. But when he came back to the starting place, the mouse was sitting on a hillock, fanning herself with her paws.

"It's very hot," she said, "to race on a day like this."

The hare was astonished. Was it possible that the mouse had beaten him?

"Let's race again," he said to the mouse.

They ran again. And again the mouse went only as far as the hummock, while the hare ran to the small hill.

They ran a third time—the hare to the hill and back, the mouse only to the first hummock.

After the third time the hare came running back worn out, his mouth open, his eyes staring. He could barely breathe from fatigue. And the mouse was sitting on the hillock again. She was laughing at the hare, laughing out loud, pointing at him with her paws.

"Some winner!" she shouted. "Couldn't even beat a mouse!"

The mouse laughed at the hare for a long time. Then she said, "I'm going to tell the other animals that I beat you. We'll have a good laugh together."

The hare became ashamed. He lay his ears back and hid in the grass. The mouse ran off.

Since then the hare always lays back his ears whenever he hears a noise or a rustle. He thinks the other animals are coming to laugh at him.

Little Elga

All this happened a long time ago. So long ago that the oldest Udege alive now hadn't even been born then. His grandfather told him about it. And the grandfather's father had told him. It was a very long time ago.

The wife of Soldiga, the hunter, died and left him with a daughter named Elga.

Soldiga buried his wife; he grieved for a while, and then he married for a second time. He took a wife from the Puning clan. And the three began to live together—Soldiga, his wife Puninga, and his daughter Elga.

Soldiga loved his daughter very much. He made her all kinds of toys: a little cradle, bowls of birch bark, a brake and a paddle for softening leather. He made the kind of toys that would help Elga get used to woman's work.

But little Elga asked her father, "Will you make me a little dog sled, a bow, arrows, and a spear?"

Puninga, hearing this, said, "Why do you want boys' toys?"

Elga answered, "When I grow up I will help father hunt."

"Is that so!" said Puninga. "That's not your work."

Soldiga looked at his daughter and saw that she was a brave little girl. So he made different toys for his daughter: a little dog sled, a small crossbow, a spear; and he carved a little reindeer and a team of little dogs out of wood.

Puninga saw that her husband didn't listen to her, and she began to dislike Elga. She started hurting her whenever the father was away hunting. Elga bore it and didn't complain to her father about her stepmother, not wanting to upset him.

And so they lived.

One day Soldiga met a boar in the taiga. Soldiga chased him for a long time—he wore him out. The boar went into the thicket and lay down exhausted.

A tiger was passing by. He was hungry. He came upon the boar and began to tear him to pieces. Soldiga couldn't quite see who was scrambling in the thicket, and he hurled his spear into it. The spear pierced the boar and grazed the tiger.

The tiger went wild and attacked Soldiga. The hunter tried to explain to the tiger that he hadn't meant to kill him—that he had been aiming at the boar. But the tiger didn't stop to listen, and he tore Soldiga to pieces.

The tiger thus learned the taste of human blood. He started coming to the village. Other hunters, Soldiga's kinsmen, went out to him and asked him not to bother them; they asked him to go somewhere else. But the tiger didn't listen to them. He started coming to the village at night—to steal pigs, reindeer, and dogs. He even started stealing little children. What could be worse?

After Elga had lost her father, life became miserable for her. Puninga hated her. She worked her to death. Elga fetched the water, washed the grain for cereal, salted the fish, dried the fish for the dogs, softened the pelts, embroidered the robes for her stepmother, brought the kindling from the taiga for the hearth. And Puninga lay on her bunk all day—eating, sleeping, smoking her

pipe, and doing nothing herself, except for yelling at Elga. "Hand me this, girl, hand me that!"

Elga knew that you had to obey your elders, so she did everything her stepmother ordered her to do. It was very hard for her. But she bore it patiently. She consoled herself, "When I grow up I will leave my stepmother. I will live by myself. I will hunt."

Elga would not part with her spear, because her father had made it. She had loved him very much. Wherever she went, she took the spear with her.

One day the stepmother sent Elga to get some birch bark for new bowls. The little girl went to the taiga, found a good birch tree, made two cuts in it, and started to strip the bark. Suddenly she heard someone asking her in a rough voice, "Hey, what are you doing here? Whose girl are you?"

Elga turned and saw the tiger. He had not caught much game for a long time. His sides were sunken in from hunger, and he was very mean. But Elga wasn't frightened of the tiger. She answered, "I am Soldiga's daughter. What do you want?"

The tiger answered, "I tore Soldiga to pieces—and now I will eat you!"

Elga shouted at the tiger, "Go away, you thief!"

The tiger sprang at Elga. The little girl ran behind the birch tree. The birch tree bent down and shielded her. The tiger slammed against the birch tree and cracked his head.

Elga threatened him with her spear. "Go away, thief, or it will be bad for you!"

The tiger roared so loudly that the leaves flew off the trees. He sprang at her again. But this time two birches moved toward each other and gripped him between them. The tiger was stuck; he couldn't get out. No matter how he struggled, he couldn't get out of the trap—that's how firmly the birches held him between them. Elga threw her spear at him. The spear went into one eye of the tiger and came out the other. Elga had blinded the tiger, and he died.

Elga chopped off the tiger's striped tail and went back to the village with it.

She saw that the people were packing their things into sacks and taking their yurts apart. They were getting ready to move because they were afraid of the tiger.

Elga said, "Where are you going? The tiger will not come any more!"

"What do you know, girl!" the oldest Udege said. "Wherever a tiger has come once, there he will come again. None of us will escape death!"

Elga showed the old man the tiger's striped tail. "I say that the tiger will not come here any more! You see, I chopped off his tail."

The Udege people became frightened.

"What did you do, little girl!" they shouted. "You mustn't kill a tiger. Now his spirit will come to the village at night and destroy us all! The taiga will come to our village—all the paths will grow over with grass. The swamp will cover this land."

Elga said, "I know the law of the hunters. I asked the tiger to leave twice. He didn't listen."

"Well, then, that's an entirely different matter," the old men said. "It's the tiger's own fault!"

The Udege didn't leave the village, and they praised the little girl.

Puninga was jealous that she wasn't the one who was praised. She became furious with Elga. No matter what the little girl did, she couldn't please Puninga. If Elga washed the grain and started to cook the cereal, the stepmother came over, threw away the grain, and made her start over again. If Elga embroidered a robe, the stepmother didn't like it.

"What are you doing, clumsy girl!" she said. "Is this the way to embroider? Rip it out and do it all over. Make it prettier, more colorful, more intricate."

Puninga kept shouting and yelling at her. Elga began to cry. She went out of the yurt to the riverbank and sat down with her embroidery near some ferns. As she sat crying, with the robe lying next to her, the ferns began to rustle and stir.

One of the ferns asked Elga, "Why are you crying, little one?"

Elga told them how hard her life was. The fern patted her with his feathery leaves and said, "Don't cry, little one! Your trouble is easy to fix. We will help you."

The fern called all the flowers and grasses together to help Elga. All the different grasses came to where the robe was lying. They lay down on top of it and twisted themselves into all kinds of patterns. Elga had never seen such a beautiful design as was made on that robe!

Then the fern gathered all of Elga's tears and sprinkled them onto the robe, and the tears fixed the design on it.

The fern said to Elga, "We care about you, Elga! Your stepmother has hurt you so much and you have cried so much that all this ground has been soaked through with your tears, and we have grown up on your tears. That's why we help you now as much as we can."

Elga carried the robe back to the village.

Many good embroiderers lived there, but when they saw the design on Elga's robe, their mouths fell open from envy and astonishment. Never had there been such a robe anywhere!

But Puninga became even more furious with Elga.

"I want a robe embroidered with reindeer hair!" she said to Elga.

But it was summer, when the reindeer's hair is short. Where was one to get long hair for embroidery?

Elga walked all over the village, asked all her neighbors, but no one could help her.

Elga sat down and began to cry again. To console herself, she started to caress the toys her father had made for her. She recalled her father fondly, and her tears flowed even more.

Suddenly the toy reindeer, which her father had made for her, said to the little girl, "Don't cry, mistress, your troubles can be eased!"

He shook himself, he stamped on the ground with his little feet, and he began to grow. He grew and grew, until he became big. He was covered with thick, white winter hair. He threw off his coat of hair and became little again.

Elga made a new robe. The hair pricked her hands badly. But the stepmother still wasn't pleased.

Puninga said, "It's not you who is doing this! Somebody is helping you. Only it won't do you any good. You will never embroider as well as I. I'll embroider a robe for myself, and then you will see what can be done! Run over to the village on the Anyuy River. My grandmother lives there. Ask her to give you my needle. And make sure you return by morning—don't be late!"

It was far to the village on the Anyuy River—it took several days to walk there.

What was Elga to do? She grew sad again. She began caressing her toys again, recalling her father fondly. Suddenly she heard a voice. "Don't be sad, little mistress, what are we for?"

Elga looked around. Before her stood a whole team of little dogs. Twelve little dogs, one more beautiful than the next! Their fur was white, their eyes yellow, and their noses black. They wagged their bushy little tails. They stamped their slender little feet. Elga was astonished.

"Where are you from?" she asked the little dogs.

And they answered, "Don't you recognize us, Elga? Soldiga made us."

Elga looked and saw that where the little toy dogs had been now stood

live ones, real ones. They had heard their mistress crying and had come to life.

Elga harnessed her little dogs to a sled and got onto it. The little dogs tore off at a gallop. Over the forest, over the river they flew in a straight line! The little girl closed her eyes. The little dogs had already risen up to the clouds. Elga opened her eyes. She saw it was light all around. The clouds were lying about her like fluffy snow. Elga took up the reins and began to drive the sled.

"Takh, takh!" she shouted. "Pot-pot-pot!"

Tufts of clouds flew from under the little dogs' feet. Before Elga even had time to get tired and cold, the dogs had brought her to the Anyuy village.

Elga got off the sled. She found Puninga's grandmother. The old woman was lying on her bunk sick, unwashed, uncombed. Elga felt sorry for the old woman, so she washed her and combed her hair. She found a little ginseng root and gave it to the grandmother to munch. The grandmother ate the little root and became well. She said to Elga, "Thank you, little girl! You are good! You did me a kindness. And I will repay you with kindness. My granddaughter wants not her needle but your death. I will give you the needle, but when you give it to her, see that you hold it with the eye toward you."

The sun had barely climbed out of the sea when Elga returned home on her little dog sled.

The stepmother was sitting there, as furious as could be.

"Well," she said, "where is my needle?"

"Here it is," said Elga. "Here is the needle."

As she started to hand the needle to the stepmother, she remembered what the old woman had told her. She turned the needle with its eye toward herself and with the point toward the stepmother.

But the needle turned out to be not just an ordinary needle. As soon as Puninga took it in her hand, it began to shuttle between her fingers: it sewed right through her fingers, sewing them to each other. No matter how hard Puninga tried, she couldn't separate her fingers.

"Well, you've out-tricked me, girl!" she said to Elga.

Now she realized who was helping Elga. She waited for Elga to fall asleep. Then she made a fire in the hearth. She threw all the toys that Elga's father had made for her into the fire. She threw in the reindeer, she threw in the little dogs. They began to burn. But one little dog jumped out of the fire, ran to Elga, nudged her with his nose, and woke her up. "Trouble, Elga! The stepmother wants to kill us all! We must run!"

"Where should we run?" Elga asked.

"We must run away from the stepmother," the little dog answered.

Elga ran out of the yurt, the little dog running after her.

Puninga saw them and dashed after them.

Just then the moon rose. A moonbeam stretched along the surface of the river, making a path. Elga and the little dog ran along the narrow path as though they were running on ice over a frozen river. Puninga hurled herself after them. But under her, the path broke—it couldn't bear her weight. The stepmother fell. She seized Elga's little spear. She flung the spear after Elga. The spear flew up to Soldiga's daughter and said, "Well, good-bye, little mistress! Now we will part!"

The spear turned back. It flew down to the stepmother. It went into one of her eyes and came out the other, and then shattered into dust. Puninga's eyes became as big as saucers. Puninga flapped her arms, and they became wings. Big claws grew on her feet. And the stepmother became a goggle-eyed owl. She wanted to return home, but her wings carried her to the taiga. She perched in a tree and yelled, "Pu-nin-ga! Pu-nin-ga!"

And this is how the owl cries to this day.

Elga and the little dog ran and ran along the moonbeam path and finally came to the moon. The little girl wanted to go back, but it began to grow light and the moonbeam path disappeared. So the little girl and the little dog remained on the moon.

Each day toward morning Elga comes down to earth. She drops into every house and looks at everything, searching for Soldiga's spear. She shines a light on every weapon—to see if Soldiga's spear is there. And if she sees a sleeping child with tears in its eyes, Elga wipes the tears and makes a gift of a pleasant dream, so that the child forgets its hurt. This is why children do not remember being hurt.

But when the owl in the taiga cries "Pu-nin-ga! Pu-nin-ga!" Elga quickly runs back.

You can see her at night if you open your eyes when the light of the moon touches them.

The Fox and the Bear

How can you trust someone who is crafty? A crafty person has one thing on his tongue and another on his mind. If you take up with someone crafty, watch him with both eyes!

Once a fox lived in the taiga. She was very clever and very crafty. And she lived in clover. She caught pheasants, quail, and woodcocks. Though she hunted birds, she didn't scorn fledglings. And as for eggs, did she love them! How many nests she destroyed and how many fledglings she killed cannot be counted. A cuckoo once started to count. "Cu-ckoo! One. Cu-ckoo! Two"—and she is still counting. The fox plundered so much that game began to disappear in that part of the taiga.

But time passes, and misfortune came to the fox too. She grew old; she began to see poorly, to have less strength. One day she went hunting. She saw a pheasant cock walking along the path. She sneaked up to him, jumped out of the bushes, and grabbed him! But the pheasant began to struggle and flutter and beat his wings. He scratched the fox's tender nose with his spurs until it bled, and he got away. The fox couldn't manage him. The pheasant flew onto a bush and started to laugh at the fox.

"Eh, you!" he said. "You shouldn't be hunting. You should be a pelt! You aren't good for anything else any more!"

The fox began to cry from hunger and rage. She trudged off to her lair.

She wandered over the taiga all day long but couldn't catch anything. She even tried picking lingonberries. She munched on them for a while and became very depressed. There was much to eat, but nothing to fill up on.

That autumn the migrating birds started to leave for warm parts early. Formations of ducks and geese and cranes stretched across the sky. They shouted as they flew: they were saying good-bye until spring to the hills, to the taiga, to the taiga lakes.

When the fox heard these shouts, she thought that now she would surely die. The snow would come early, and she hadn't stored any supplies for the winter.

The fox wandered around aimlessly with her head hanging low.

"I will look for someone more stupid than I," she said. "If I find someone, maybe somehow I'll make it through the winter."

She met a bear and asked him, "Where are you going, neighbor?"

The bear answered, "I'm looking for someone, neighbor, to tell me what the cranes are shouting about at night."

The fox thought a while, then answered, "We'll have to make some magic like a shaman. That's how we'll find out."

The fox put on a bast belt and tied little wood chips and stones onto it. She started to dance, swishing her tail and beating on a dog skull instead of a tambour. The bear listened open-mouthed as he watched the fox. He clapped his palms, helping the fox make magic.

The fox twirled and twirled, and then she said, "Well, neighbor, I have found out what the cranes shout about at night."

"What, then?"

"They shout that this will be an early winter, cold and long. They shout that all the animals must help one another. They shout that even a lair will not save you from such a hard winter!"

The bear became frightened.

"Then what should we do?" he asked.

The crafty fox answered him, "We'll have to live together. It is warmer when there are two. And now," she said, "we must collect supplies for the winter and take them to the lair!"

The bear thought, what did he need supplies for when sucking his paw was enough for him for the whole winter? And that's what he told the fox. The fox became angry and began to shout at the bear and stamp her feet. "Who was it that wanted to find out what the cranes were shouting about? You. And now that you have found out, do what you are told. If you won't, I'll find another companion for myself for the winter! And you can perish all by yourself."

The bear begged the fox not to be angry, and she relented.

They agreed to live together. They started to put in a supply of food. They went hunting, but it went badly. The fox had no strength, and the bear became sleepy. He was looking for game but really thinking of his lair. What kind of hunting was that?

The fox became furious, but she didn't show it. She kept walking and trying to figure out how to trick the bear.

They wandered around the taiga for a long time, but they had no luck.

Suddenly the bear raised his snout. The fur on the back of his neck stood up straight, he opened his nostrils and his eyes wide, he sniffed the air, and he said, "I smell a stranger's smell, neighbor!"

He started to grope around with his paw, and he raked something up.

The fox saw a hunting knife in the bear's paw. Someone must have been hunting and dropped a knife. The fox began to sing in a small, thin voice and to dance, as though for joy. The bear asked what she was so happy about.

The fox answered, "Why shouldn't I be happy, neighbor? Now we will live through the winter without trouble. This thing that you found is magical. By itself it can get you more meat than you could catch in a whole hunting season!"

The bear was happy too. Now he wouldn't have to trudge all over the taiga, now he could go to sleep in his lair.

"Let's go home quickly, neighbor," he said.

"Yes, let's!"

The fox ran ahead. She ran to a path on the slope of a hill. She stuck the knife, blade up, in the middle of the path and came back. She shouted to the bear, "Why are you walking so slowly? You have to run."

They ran until they reached the slope.

Then the fox said, "Let's roll down the hill. Let's see who can roll the fastest!"

The bear agreed. So they rolled down head over heels.

The fox was rolling and singing, "Roll, roll, piece of meat!"

"What are you singing?" the bear asked the fox.

"I am singing that there is enough meat now for a quarter of the winter."

They rolled on. The fox sang again. The bear asked her what she was singing now.

The fox answered, "I am singing, neighbor, that there is enough meat now for half the winter."

The bear rolled and struck the knife that the fox had stuck in the path, and it ripped his belly open.

At this the fox sang at the top of her voice, "Lie, lie, piece of meat!"

The bear groaned and asked the fox, "And what are you singing now?"

"I am singing, neighbor, that there is enough meat for the whole winter now."

The bear died. The fox carried the bear meat into the bear's lair. She spent the winter there.

That is how the fox tricked the bear.

They are right when they say that nothing good can be expected from a cheat and a swindler!

A Sure Sign

In a village there lived a couple, Churka and Pigunayka. Churka was a quiet man—he didn't talk much. But his wife Pigunayka worked more with her tongue than with her hands. She even talked in her sleep. She would be sleeping, and suddenly she would start muttering—so fast you couldn't understand a word of what she said. Churka would be awakened by his wife's yelling, and he'd give her a shove in the side. "Hey, wife, who are you talking to?"

Pigunayka would jump up and rub her eyes with her fist. "I am talking with some smart people."

"But you're dreaming, wife!"

"It's nice to talk with smart people, even in your dreams. After all, I

151

can't talk with you! You say all of two words a year, and those only when you're away in the taiga."

There were three things that Churka did: hunt animals, catch fish, and smoke his pipe. He did all of them very well. When Churka hunted animals in the taiga, he would chase after them until his friends had to lead him out of the taiga by force. When Churka went fishing, he would go wild and climb right into the net himself if the fish were not coming. And when Churka lighted his pipe, the smoke would rise as thick as clouds, right up to the sky! If Churka was smoking at home, people would come running from the whole village. Where was the fire? They came running, but saw it was only Churka sitting on his doorstep, smoking his pipe. And if Churka was in the taiga, when the Nivkhs saw smoke rising in clouds above the taiga, they would know that Churka had lighted his pipe that was as thick as a man's leg! How many times they were mistaken when they thought a forest fire was only smoke from Churka's pipe!

There were also three things that Pigunayka did: talk, sleep, and interpret dreams. She did all of them very well. When she started to talk, she out-talked everybody; her neighbors would hide from her under their bunks. Their only salvation was to place the old deaf woman Koynyt next to Pigunayka. Koynyt would sit and nod her head, as though agreeing, while Pigunayka talked. And when Pigunayka fell asleep, no one could wake her until she had finished all her dreaming. Once while she was asleep some neighbor boys carried her, together with her bedding, to the forest. When she awoke there, looked around, and saw the forest, she thought she was dreaming. She said to herself, "I am so stupid! Why am I dreaming sitting up? I should be lying down." So she lay down and slept for two more weeks. The same boys had to carry her back home. And when Pigunayka started interpreting dreams, she said such frightful things that old women would fall out of their bunks at night afterwards! They didn't know whether what Pigunayka said would come to pass, but they trembled for a whole week after her interpretations. Nobody could interpret dreams better than Pigunayka.

One morning when she woke up, she lay quietly, not saying anything. Churka looked at his wife and became frightened. Why wasn't she saying anything? Had something happened?

"What's the matter, Pigunayka?" he asked.

"I dreamed of a red berry," his wife said. "That means a quarrel."

"Why, wife? Why should we quarrel?"

"It means a quarrel," Pigunayka said. "It is a sure sign. Don't I know how to interpret dreams? Do you remember, I once dreamed of reindeer meat, and I said it meant a blizzard. Wasn't there a blizzard after that?"

Churka didn't say anything. He didn't want to say that his wife had dreamed of reindeer meat after the snow had already blocked their door; when he and his wife had woken up, they couldn't open the door and had to stay in the house for three days. It was only on the third day that his wife dreamed of reindeer meat.

"Why don't you say something?" Pigunayka said. "A red berry means a quarrel—that I know well."

"I am not going to quarrel with you, Pigunayka," Churka muttered. His wife became angry.

"What do you mean, you won't, after I had such a dream!"

"What should I quarrel for?"

"You'll find out what for! Maybe you'll remember how our fish went bad, when I lay down for a minute."

"That's true, wife. The fish did go bad. You slept for three whole days that time. They were barely able to wake you when our bunk caught on fire because coals had been left in the hearth unattended."

"Aha!" said Pigunayka. "So your wife can't even lie down? She has to look after you all the time. That's the kind of man you are!"

"Wife," said Churka, "why talk about it? The fish went bad—it's all right. Afterwards I caught twice as many."

"Aha," said Pigunayka, "you're reproaching me again! You want me to go fishing for you? I see you want to quarrel with me!"

"Wife, I don't want to quarrel," Churka said.

"Yes, you do!" his wife said. "If I dreamed of a red berry, we have to quarrel!"

"I don't want to!" said Churka.

"Yes, you do!"

"I don't!"

"You do—I can see it in your eyes!"

"Wife!" said Churka, raising his voice.

"Ah, so you're starting to shout at me?" said Pigunayka and banged her husband on the forehead with a ladle!

Churka was a quiet man, but when he saw that a lump the size of a fist had grown on his forehead, he fought back.

They grabbed each other.

Pigunayka shouted, "We have to quarrel!"

"No, we don't!"

"Yes, we do!"

"No, we don't!"

They made as much noise as the blizzard had the time Pigunayka dreamed of reindeer meat.

Neighbors from the whole village came running. The men tried to pull Churka back, while the women held on to Pigunayka. They pulled and pulled, but they couldn't separate them. They brought some water from the river, and they tried to separate husband and wife by pouring it on them.

"Eh, wife," Churka said, "wait! Our roof must have gotten a hole in it. It's raining!"

The neighbors finally separated them.

Churka sat down and counted his lumps. Pigunayka sat down and rubbed her swollen eyes with her hands.

"What happened?" the neighbors asked them.

"Nothing," Pigunayka said. "It's just that I dreamed I was picking red berries. That's a sure sign—it means a quarrel!"

Who would know better than Pigunayka—she did dream of a red berry, and she did quarrel with her husband!

The Stupid Rich Man

Wealth does not bring brains. And greed takes away whatever brains there may be.

Two men lived on the Amur: a Chinese merchant, Li-Fu, and a Nanai hunter, Aktanka. The two were very different. Aktanka fished and hunted; he had worked all his life, but still he was poor. Li-Fu couldn't put an arrow to a bow, couldn't tell a jay from a grouse, hadn't caught a single fish in his whole life, and didn't even know what a net was. All he did was trade in his store and count his money, but he was rich. Aktanka gave him his whole catch in return for grain and flour.

Li-Fu was a greedy and dishonest man. He took furs from Aktanka. He wrote down everything he took in and everything he gave out in his fat book. But he always wrote it down wrong. Aktanka could neither read nor write, so he couldn't figure out for himself how much he owed Li-Fu.

And so it would happen that the more successful Aktanka's hunt was, the more Li-Fu's goods would cost.

And Aktanka could never pay off what he owed.

Every day Li-Fu would come running to Aktanka's house, shouting, "Hey, you! Don't lie there! Get up! Go hunting! You have a debt to pay!"

One day Li-Fu took Aktanka's net as payment for what was owed him. His greed had made him so stupid that he didn't understand that Aktanka couldn't catch any fish without his net.

Aktanka thought and thought. He thought for a long time. Then he made a snare of elk sinew; he set the snare and a crossbow up on the path that the boar took to his watering place. When the boar went to drink, the crossbow killed him. Aktanka had a catch again.

He started to cook the meat.

Li-Fu smelled the meat cooking and came running. He shouted at the hunter, stamped his feet, and pointed his finger at his fat book. "Hey, you, pay your debt!"

So Aktanka gave him all his meat. But even this wasn't enough for Li-Fu. He also wanted to take both the crossbow and the snare! That's what he wanted.

Ainka, Aktanka's wife, said, "What will we do, Mr. Li-Fu? Without weapons and snares there can't be any catch; there can be neither meat nor pelts."

But Li-Fu didn't listen to her; he grabbed everything and left. Ainka began to cry.

Aktanka said to her, "Never mind, wife, we'll manage somehow."

He thought and thought. He thought for a long time. Then he made a small bow out of a yew-tree branch and went to the taiga.

Aktanka's eye was sharp and his hand steady. Every time he shot an arrow, he killed a bird. He killed a great deal of game. He brought it home. Ainka started to roast the birds on a spit.

Greedy Li-Fu again smelled something roasting at Aktanka's yurt, so again he came running. "Pay your debt!"

Aktanka couldn't pay his debt. Li-Fu took the birds and the small bow with its arrows. And he left.

Ainka cried. "Oy-ya-kha! How will we live now?"

Aktanka said to her, "Don't cry, wife, let us think for a while. It's better to think than to cry."

Aktanka started to think. He thought all night. He smoked up almost all his tobacco while he thought.

In the morning he said to his wife, "Go prepare some pitch."

Ainka went into the forest. She collected pitch from the spruce and other fir trees. She collected a great deal of it. Then she boiled it and stirred it.

Aktanka took a birchbark bowl, filled it with pitch, and went to a cliff where a tall spruce stood.

He climbed the tree to its very top. He looked around. He saw birds flying. Aktanka then climbed down the tree, smearing the pitch on the trunk and branches above him as he came down. He climbed down and smeared, climbed down and smeared, until he had covered the whole tree with pitch; then he went home to sleep.

In the morning he awakened his wife. "Hey, wife, go collect the catch!"

Aktanka's wife went to the tree. She saw that the whole tree was covered with birds. At night the birds had come to rest on the tree and had gotten stuck in the pitch. No matter how hard they flapped their wings, they couldn't pull themselves away. Ainka collected the game and took it home. She started to roast the birds.

Li-Fu was sleeping and counting profits in his dreams. Suddenly there was again a smell of roasting meat coming from Aktanka's yurt. He jumped up and ran. He was shaking all over with greed: his hands were trembling, his pigtail was bouncing on his back, his slippers were falling off his feet, and his robe was flapping above his knees.

Li-Fu came running to Aktanka's yurt, pointing his finger at his fat book. "Hey!" he shouted. "You don't pay your debt, but you are eating meat! Pay your debt!"

"I can't," said Aktanka. "I can't, Mr. Li-Fu."

"Then give me your gear!"

"I don't have any gear," Aktanka said. "You yourself took all my things."

Li-Fu thrust his hand into Aktanka's pot and pulled out a duck. When he saw the bird, he opened his eyes wide, stamped his feet, turned red with rage, and shouted in a voice not his own. "And did this duck fly into your pot by itself?"

"I caught it without any weapons," Aktanka answered. "All you have to do is smear a tree with pitch. Birds will perch on the tree and get stuck; then you simply pick them off with your bare hands and throw them into the pot."

Li-Fu became happy. "That is good," he thought. "Now I will catch all the geese and all the ducks! Business will be good, the store will do well. And I won't give any flour or grain or lard to Aktanka any more!"

The rich man ran home. He sent his wife to the forest to collect pitch. The rich man's wife collected a whole barrelful of pitch. The two of them together could barely carry the barrel up to the hill where the tall trees stood.

Li-Fu put some pitch into a copper pot and began to climb up the tree. He climbed up and smeared, climbed up and smeared.

By the time he reached the top, he had smeared the whole tree. He smeared it very thickly, so that even more birds would get stuck to it.

His wife shouted to him from below, "Hey, Li-Fu, climb down now or you'll scare away all the birds. Look, a whole flock of geese is flying this way! They're so fat that their fat is dripping from them into the river!"

The merchant started to climb down. But the tree was sticky. The lower he climbed, the stickier the pitch was.

Li-Fu got stuck to the tree. His arms, his legs, and his embroidered robe all got stuck.

His wife was hurrying him. "Climb down quickly, Li-Fu! The geese are already close."

But Li-Fu couldn't move up or down. He said to his wife, "I can't climb down! Chop down the tree! The birds will also perch on a felled tree."

The rich man's wife seized an ax and started chopping down the tree. She kept swinging with all her might—all you could see was wood chips flying in all directions.

And Li-Fu kept shouting, "Hurry, hurry! Or the geese will fly away!"

The wife chopped down the tree. It fell and hit the ground; greedy Li-Fu was killed. A branch broke off and struck the rich man's wife on the forehead, and she fell into the barrel of pitch; the barrel fell over onto its side and rolled down the hill and into the river, carrying the wife of the stupid and greedy Li-Fu with it. Don't feel sorry for her—she was no better than her husband!

Aktanka went into Li-Fu's house and took back all his gear: the small bow, the crossbow, and the snare. Now he could live—once again he could hunt and fish.

And no one took his catch away from him any more.

Two Weak Ones Against
One Strong One

One weak one against one strong one is like a mouse against a bear: the bear has only to bring his paw down, and there'll be no more mouse! But with two weak ones against one strong one—there we would have to see who came out ahead!

There was once a bear who completely forgot the law of the taiga: he started making mischief and hurting small animals. He made life impossible for the mice, the gophers, and the weasels. He made life impossible for the marmots, the gerbils, and the polecats. No one could have blamed the bear if he had been tempted to kill them because he was hungry. But he was full! And fat! He killed not so much for eating as for the sake of killing. He simply liked to chase the small animals. And you couldn't hide from him anywhere: if you hid in a hollow tree, he would get you; in a lair, he would get you; on a branch, he would get you; and in the water, he would get you!

The animals cried, but they didn't do anything about it. Then the bear started killing their babies. That was a terrible thing, a most evil thing— you couldn't think of anything worse! The bear started destroying birds' nests and killing baby animals in their lairs.

He killed all the little mouse's children. He brought his foot down on them once—and not one was left alive. The mouse cried and dashed around wildly. But what could she do against the bear by herself?

The bear destroyed the little titmouse's nest and ate all the eggs. The titmouse cried, and flew around and around her nest. But what could she do against the bear by herself?

And the bear just laughed at them.

The mouse ran to look for protection. She heard the titmouse crying. The mouse asked, "Hey, neighbor, what happened? Why are you crying?"

The titmouse answered, "The time had just come for my children to hatch! They were already tapping with their little beaks on the shells. And the bear gobbled them all up! Where will I find protection? What can I do by myself?"

The mouse too began to cry. "Black fur was already beginning to cover my children. They were already starting to open their little eyes! And the bear killed them all too!"

Where could they find protection? How could they save their children from the bear? It was very far to the home of the Master of the Taiga. And neither animal had enough strength to punish the bear by herself. They thought and thought, and finally decided on a plan. "Why should we be afraid?" they said. "There are two of us now!"

They went to look for the bear. But the bear was coming toward them himself. He was walking, waddling from side to side. From force of habit, he raised his paw as soon as he saw them. He was about to kill the mouse and the titmouse, to crush them both with a single blow.

But the titmouse shouted to him, "Hey, neighbor, wait! I have some good news!"

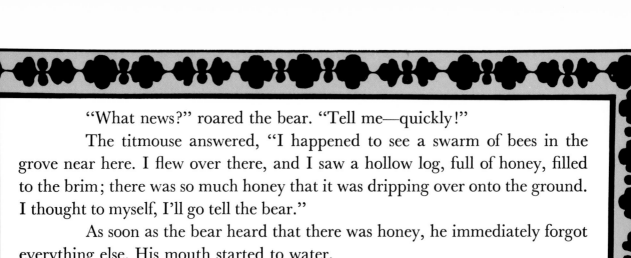

"What news?" roared the bear. "Tell me—quickly!"

The titmouse answered, "I happened to see a swarm of bees in the grove near here. I flew over there, and I saw a hollow log, full of honey, filled to the brim; there was so much honey that it was dripping over onto the ground. I thought to myself, I'll go tell the bear."

As soon as the bear heard that there was honey, he immediately forgot everything else. His mouth started to water.

"And where is that log?" he asked the titmouse.

"We'll take you there, neighbor," the mouse said to him.

So they started off.

The titmouse flew in front, showing the way, but leading the bear the long way around, while the mouse ran straight to the grove.

She ran up to the log and shouted to the bees, "Hey, neighbors, I have important business with you!"

The bees came flying out to her. The mouse told them about her business.

The bees said to her, "How can we not help in this matter? We certainly will help! This bear has done much harm to us too—how many hives has he crushed!"

The titmouse brought the bear to the grove. She showed him where the log lay. But the bear already saw it himself; he dashed toward it, licking his lips, snorting, and puffing. As soon as the bear reached the log, the whole swarm of bees flew at him. They started stinging him on all sides! The bear tried to drive them away by waving his paw at them, but the bees kept going at him. The bear roared and darted back. But his eyes were so swollen from the bee stings that they were completely closed. The bear couldn't see the road. He ran straight over all the gullies, all the dead trees and branches. He was tripping and falling, and he got so scratched up he was bleeding. And still the bees kept after him!

Only one thing could save the bear—throwing himself into water and sitting there until the bees flew away. But the bear's eyes were so swollen that he couldn't see where he was running. Then he remembered the mouse and the titmouse. He shouted with all his might, "Hey, neighbors, where are you?"

"Here we are!" the mouse and the titmouse answered. "The bees are eating us all up—we are dying!"

"Lead me to water!" shouted the bear.

The titmouse perched on the bear's right shoulder, the mouse jumped

onto the other. The bear was howling. The two neighbors told him where to turn, where to run, and where to climb over the dead trees.

The titmouse said to him, "We can already see the river, neighbor."

The mouse said to him, "Now it's quite close, neighbor."

"That's good!" said the bear. "The cursed bees have bitten me all up! The farther we go, the worse they sting!"

He couldn't see that the bees had long since fallen behind.

Then the mouse and the titmouse shouted to him, "Jump into the water, neighbor, and sit down on the bottom. It is shallow here!"

The bear thought to himself, "Let me just get rid of the bees, and then I'll leave nothing of you, neighbors, but a wet spot!"

The bear jumped with all his might.

He thought he was jumping into a river, but he had leaped into a gorge, where the mouse and the titmouse had led him. The bear was falling down a precipice, knocking against one cliff and then another. His fur was flying in all directions.

The titmouse flew along, next to the falling bear. "You thought you were so strong, bear, that no power could be found to stand up against you. You ate my children!"

The mouse was sitting on the bear—she had burrowed into his fur. She said, "You thought you were so strong, bear, that no power could be found to stand up against you. You killed my children!"

The bear crashed to the ground and died.

It served him right! Why did he kill animal babies?

Small animals and birds came running from everywhere. They bowed to the mouse and to the titmouse; they thanked them.

What can one weak one do against one strong one?

But with two weak ones against one strong one—we have to see who comes out ahead!

Greedy Kanchuga

All these things happened when animals could still understand human language. In those days the tiger was kin to the Udege people. In those days the tiger was a welcome guest in the Bisanka clan.

The Bisankas lived at the headwaters of the Koppi River. There were many, many Bisankas, and when they all spoke at once, their voices could be heard as far away as the Anyuy River.

One year they had a very good hunting season. The hunters killed more sable, otter, squirrel, weasel, polecat, bear, and fox than ever before.

Merchants came to the Bisankas and bought many of their furs. But even after the merchants had taken all the furs they wanted, the Bisankas' supply did not seem to have diminished at all.

The Bisankas decided to go to the Amur and sell the rest of their furs there. They outfitted twenty dog sleds, picking the best dogs in the village. They put on their best clothes. They bound their braids with new, red ribbons. They put on hats of musk-deer pelts with sable tails; they put white bands on their heads. They put on white robes embroidered with silk, and white trousers. They sat down on their sleds, raised their riding sticks, then put them away between the sled runners, giving their dogs free rein.

"Takh, takh! Pot-pot-pot!"

The dogs took off. All you could see was the snow flying in all directions, and all you could hear was the squeaking of the sled runners.

The dogs barked as they ran. Hearing that bark, the wild animals ran off in all directions—they hid behind trees and snowbanks. The dogs flew like the wind.

They were such good dogs that they ran without stopping. They even ate their dried fish on the run.

The dogs ran over the top of a mountain—it was nothing to them. They dashed in a straight line over mountains, rivers, hollows. They came to the headwaters of the Anyuy River; from there they ran on to the Khor River, then to the Ussuri River, and at last to the Amur. How long the Udege drove—who knows? They drove merrily and didn't count the time!

There was a big market in Mullaki Town on the Amur. Many people gathered there from all about: the Nanai from the Amur; the Nivkhs, dressed in fishskins, from Sakhalin Island; the Negidals, on dog sleds, from the Amgun River; the Orochons, in sheepskins, from distant pastures; the Ulches in elkskin boots; the Oroches in reindeer boots. So many people had gathered, you couldn't count them all!

There was a great market there. Many merchants came: the pigtailed Manchus and the clean-shaven Chinese with long nails; merchants in wooden armor with two-handled swords came from faraway islands.

But with the merchants came the Black Death. Who knows by what means she came? In a boat, on a dog sled, on reindeer back, or by foot—I don't know. What she wore—I don't know either. But she became mistress in that great market.

As the Bisankas sat down to trade, misfortune struck.

The Black Death attacked the people. And they started dying. The Nanai, the Chinese, the Negidals, the Orochons, the Manchus, the Oroches, and the Ulches all started dying; the hunters and the merchants started dying.

The people saw that things were bad: death bargained with nobody at the market; she took everyone away, one by one. The people ran off in all directions.

But among the Bisankas almost no one was left to run! Of them all only one young man, named Konga, had been left alive. He had come with his brother, but the Black Death took his brother away. Konga buried his kinsmen. Then he thought, "How can I leave my brother in a strange land? Let him come with me. Let him be buried according to our custom. Let him stand before the Master for all of our kinsmen!"

Konga built a big box and laid his brother in it.

Konga left all the furs behind—this was not the time to think of them. He got into the last dog sled, shouted to the dogs, and drove as fast as he could—home, away from this cursed place!

Konga drove fast, not looking back, running away from the plague.

But the plague was lying in the box with his brother.

How long Konga drove—who knows? First on the frozen Ussuri, then on the Khor, then on the Anyuy, then over the mountains.

In those mountains there were rocky clearings. In one of these there was a tiger camp. In that camp lived tigers. Many roads led to the camp, and they were paved with bones and edged with skulls.

Konga drove up to the tigers' road.

A tiger was standing on the road. When he saw Konga, he rolled over and became a man. He said hello and asked how Konga had done at the market and what news he brought.

Konga told him what misfortune had befallen them and what bad news he was bringing with him. The tiger man shook his head and said, "Go now! I will come to your brother's funeral to cry over him. Your brother was a good hunter." He rolled over, became a tiger again, and left.

Konga crossed the road. It was not far from there to his own village.

Konga came home and told his mother and his kinsmen what had happened to him. His mother opened the box to say good-bye to the body of her son.

When she opened the box, she let out the plague.

The Black Death went roaming through the village, killing Konga, his mother, and all the people.

Only Konga's little brother and sister were left alive. And the shaman Kanchuga.

Kanchuga was cowardly and greedy. He never helped anyone with anything. He saw that, besides himself, only two children were left alive. He thought, "Until death leaves, I'll eat as much as I can and keep as much as I can for myself. Why should I help the children? If I do, there might not be enough for me."

He closed the door of Konga's yurt and leaned a heavy log against it, leaving the children in the yurt. He went into his own yurt and shut the door. And he sat in his yurt and stuffed himself.

At first he stayed in his yurt. But then he was overcome by greed.

"Why," thought Kanchuga, "should all the food in the village go to waste? You mustn't take from the dead—that is a great sin. Evil spirits guard the food of the dead," Kanchuga said to himself. "But that's all right! They are many—I am one. If they attack me, they will bump into one another, they will fight among themselves, and they will forget about me!"

So Kanchuga went to collect food from the other yurts. From all over the village he collected pickled lingonberries, seal fat, salted garlic, elk meat, sturgeon bellies, the dried roots of the day lily, and birdcherry cakes. He took all this food to his yurt. Then he sat in his yurt and stuffed himself.

And in Konga's yurt the hungry children were crying.

Then the tiger came to the village. He rolled over and became a man. He saw that no smoke was rising from the chimneys, no people were walking about, no tambour was roaring, no dogs were barking—everyone was lying dead. He had come to cry over Konga's brother, but now he needed more tears than he had ever had—there were so many corpses in the village.

The tiger man heard someone crying in Konga's yurt. He opened the door and saw the children. He took them in his arms. Then he walked around the village, looking for anyone who was still alive. Not a person answered his call.

The tiger man went up to Kanchuga's yurt. He pulled on the door—it wouldn't open. But he could hear someone moving about inside.

The tiger man knocked on the door.

Kanchuga heard the knock. He thought that Konga's children had

170

somehow gotten out of their yurt and had come to ask him for something to eat. Kanchuga kept stuffing his mouth, chewing, and choking on his food. He could hardly swallow the food, he was stuffing his mouth so much and so fast. But he shouted, "Go away, don't ask me for food—I have nothing to eat myself!"

Then the tiger man said, "Eh, Kanchuga, you have forgotten the law of the forest people: help the weak, give to the hungry, shelter the orphan! This is how the Udege have always lived. And this is how they will still live. There is no room for you among true people! You will die of fright three times. Your body will keep growing smaller and your greed greater. This is what will happen to you until you disappear altogether!"

He rolled over and became a tiger. Then he put the children on his back and carried them to the tiger camp.

He said to his kinsmen, "Here are my uncle's children. There is no one to feed them."

The tigers started to feed the children. They gave them the best pieces of meat. The children began to grow. They were given new names, so that the Black Death couldn't follow them by their old names to the new place on the trail. They called the girl Inga and the boy Yegda.

In a short time the children grew up.

Inga became a needlewoman, Yegda a hunter.

When the time came, the old tiger crossed the tigers' road with them and showed them the people's road. He told them what the law was and how to live so that all would go well. Then he went back to his camp.

And Inga and Yegda went back to their own people.

They walked past their father's old village. The paths to the village were overgrown with grass. Yegda tied a bunch of dried grass and hung it over the path, so people would go by without stopping.

That is what happened to the children.

And this is what happened to Kanchuga. As soon as the tiger man had finished speaking to him, Kanchuga's nose grew long, two tusks pushed their way out of his mouth, bristles grew on his back, and hooves grew on his hands and feet. Kanchuga became a wild boar. He became smaller, but his greed became greater. He gobbled up everything in his yurt. Then he ran into the taiga. He dug up roots and devoured them. He gnawed the young grass. He searched for acorns and gulped them down. He choked from greed—but still he couldn't get enough to eat. He walked about the taiga all day long, chewing, crunching, and gnawing, but still he was hungry. Even in his sleep he smacked his lips, snorted, and chewed. He dreamed of acorns, birds' entrails, and all other kinds of food. As soon as he woke up he started eating again, but his belly always felt empty!

This was how Inga and Yegda found him in the taiga when they were coming back from the tiger people.

When Kanchuga saw the brother and sister, he thought, "I will eat them up—finally I will have enough!" Then he rushed at Konga's kinsmen.

Yegda raised his spear—and the boar-Kanchuga died of fright. He rolled over and became a lynx. Then he opened his mouth wide, bared his teeth, and again rushed at Yegda. He still wanted to eat him up.

Yegda raised his spear again—and the lynx-Kanchuga died of fright. This time he rolled over and became a rat. He was smaller, but his greed was still greater. He opened his red eyes wide, he beat the ground with his naked tail, he bared his sharp teeth, and he rushed at Yegda, thinking, "I will eat him up—I will have enough!"

Yegda waved his hand at the rat. Kanchuga died of fright a third time. He rolled over and became a beetle—a wood borer, the kind of beetle that gobbles up hundred-year-old pine trees, turning them into dust. The beetle buzzed, spread his wings, twitched his whiskers, and twirled his legs. He came flying at Yegda, sat on his forehead, opened his mouth wide, thinking he would swallow the boy alive.

Then Yegda became angry. "If your fury doesn't subside nor your greed diminish, blame yourself and not me—I am not guilty before you!"

He said this and swatted himself on the forehead.

A wet spot was all that was left of the beetle.

Greedy Kanchuga, who grudged the children food, died completely. He perished at their hands.

And no one felt sorry.

The Little Boy Chokcho

You must stand up for yourself! You must stand up for your kinsmen! You cannot forgive someone who has hurt you!

In a Nanai village lived a man named Beldy. He had a little son named Chokcho. His son was very young—he was hardly old enough to walk.

Beldy hunted the entire winter. He brought in a great many furs. He brought in sable, and squirrel, and fox, and seal, and bear, and polecat, and wolf. Beldy looked at the furs and rejoiced. "I will go to the Chinese kingdom with my catch, to the city of San-Sing; I will sell the furs and buy food and supplies for all of next winter! I will buy a new net and a gun, some gunpowder, cartridges, and toys."

And the following summer Beldy indeed made ready to go to San-Sing.

His son begged him, "Take me with you, father!"

Beldy thought, the road is dangerous—there might be an attack by robbers. Who knows what could happen on the road?

"Why, son!" said Beldy. "How could we leave the house without a man? Who would protect your mother and sisters? You must stay home."

Then Beldy left.

A long time passed. During that time Chokcho learned to use a knife. He made things out of wood: he made a spoon and a little boat, he carved a reindeer and a bear, a dog sled and some dogs. He made many different kinds of toys. But still his father did not come back.

The leaves on the trees turned yellow, and the grass withered. But still Beldy did not come home.

Then some people came from the neighboring village.

Chokcho's mother prepared food for the visitors; she served them fish stew and dried fish.

They sat and sat, they smoked and smoked, they ate and ate, and finally they said, "We went to San-Sing together with Beldy. We traded there. We have come back."

"And where is my father?" asked Chokcho.

The neighbor villagers looked at each other.

"Your father," they said, "traded with a Manchu named Lyan. The man bought all of Beldy's furs. Then Beldy went to him to get paid, and he did not come back. Lyan turned out to be not a merchant but a robber. He took all of Beldy's furs and killed him."

"Then why didn't you help him?" asked Chokcho.

They said, "Lyan, the Manchu, had a big gang. And we were few. We could not help your father—we were afraid. Lyan's people would have caught up with us, taken all our goods, too, and killed us as well."

"You acted badly," said Chokcho.

The neighbor villagers were offended; they got into their boat and sailed away.

Chokcho's mother began to cry; his sisters cried too.

They cried so much that their eyes became all swollen.

175

"What will happen to us now?"

But nothing could be done—you could not bring Beldy back with tears. And you had to go on living. They cried and cried, and then they went to work. The older sister took a spear and went to hunt in the taiga. The younger sister got into a boat and went to fish on the Amur. The mother stayed at home, to watch over the fire and to cook the food.

Chokcho said to his mother, "Sew some boots for me and bake some cakes. I will go search for Lyan. If I find him, I will avenge my father and bring back the furs!"

His mother said, "Why, Chokcho! Where will you go? You are still little."

Chokcho looked at her. "Father said that I am a man. And men must protect their kin and take vengeance on the enemy."

The mother saw that Chokcho felt strongly about going and would not be talked out of it. She baked him cakes and sewed him boots.

Chokcho took his knife, put a hunter's band on his head, put some dried fish into a sack, and put boots on his feet. Then he said good-bye to his sisters and his mother, and left.

Chokcho walked and walked, until he came to a big forest. There was no end to this forest. The trees were very tall. The branches of the pines and the oaks rustled, and the treetops swayed. But Chokcho was not afraid. He walked through the forest, munching on a cake, playing with his knife, and singing a song. Suddenly he heard a voice.

"Where are you going, little Nanai?"

Chokcho looked around. There was nobody there. The voice called to him again. Chokcho answered, "I am going to avenge my father!"

"Help me, and I will help you! I will be your friend," the voice said.

Chokcho saw an acorn lying on top of a stone. It had fallen from a tree and had landed on the stone. It lay there, withering.

"Take me with you," said the acorn, "and I'll be useful to you."

Chokcho picked up the acorn and walked on.

He found an old campfire. He stopped to rest. He took off his boots and put his feet up. He bit into a cake. Suddenly he heard a hoarse, rasping voice.

"Where are you going, young man?"

"I am going to avenge my father!" said Chokcho. "And who are you? Where are you?"

"I am lying right next to you."

Chokcho looked and saw that right next to the campfire, in the ashes, lay a spit that hunters had used for roasting meat. Someone had thrown the spit into the fire. The spit was bent, burned, and covered with soot. Chokcho helped the spit too. He cleaned off the soot with sand and straightened it out. The spit looked like new again.

"Thanks, Chokcho! You have helped me, and I will help you. Take me with you!" said the spit to the boy.

Chokcho took the spit with him and walked on. He walked past an abandoned fishing spot, and again he heard a voice. It asked him where he was going. Chokcho answered. He saw that the voice was coming from a brake and a paddle used to beat fishskins until they were soft. Someone had hammered a nail into the brake and broken the handle of the paddle. Chokcho pulled the nail out of the brake and made a new handle for the paddle.

"Thank you, Chokcho!" they said to him. "You have helped us, and we will help you. Take us with you!"

Chokcho took the brake and the paddle. He walked on.

He walked and walked, and at last he came to a stream. The stream was wide. The road ended there. What was he to do?

Then Chokcho heard someone calling to him again.

"Hey, neighbor, help me, and I will help you! I will be your friend."

Chokcho looked and saw that the stream had washed away the bank under a birch tree. The tree had fallen into the water, onto a pike, and had trapped it. The pike lay pinned under the tree and could go neither forward nor backward. It kept thrashing its tail, but it couldn't free itself. It was losing its breath. Chokcho pushed the tree aside and freed the pike. The pike said to him, "How will you cross the stream? Sit on my back, and I'll take you across."

Chokcho sat on the pike's back. In an instant he was on the other side of the stream.

The pike said to him, "Take me with you. I'll be useful to you!"

Chokcho put the pike in his sack. He walked on.

He could already see the Amur. Suddenly Chokcho saw a ski in the grass. "What a shame," thought Chokcho. "It's a good ski, but there is only one!" And then he saw the other one. It was lying far away. Someone had thrown it into the underbrush. Chokcho was not too lazy to go get the other ski. He placed the two skis down, alongside each other, and they said to him, "You have helped us, and we will help you! Where are you going, little Nanai?"

"I am going to avenge my father!" Chokcho said. "Only I don't have too much strength—I don't know if I'll get there. It's a long way. How will I get across the Amur?"

The skis said to him, "That is nothing. Stand on us, we'll give you a ride—and you'll get there faster."

Chokcho laughed. "Whoever heard of skiing on grass?"

But he got onto the skis anyway. Then the skis grew wings. They rose into the air and flew away. And so fast! The wind almost tore the band off Chokcho's head. They flew over the Amur. The river wound under them like a blue ribbon.

The skis flew and flew. The wind whistled in Chokcho's ears. Below him rivers, villages, forests skimmed by. The wind took Chokcho's breath away.

At last the skis arrived in San-Sing.

Chokcho looked around and grew frightened.

It was such a big village—there were so many houses! Chokcho had never thought there could be so many houses in one place. They stood in rows, one after another; there were so many that you couldn't see the end of them. And there were so many people there! Their voices made as much noise as a storm felling trees. People were pushing and shouting. They were buying, bartering, and selling. There were many people, but not a one that he knew.

Chokcho tried to ask how to go to the house of Lyan the Manchu. The passersby laughed at the boy—they could not understand him. Somebody hit him, another pushed him, another pulled his braid, someone else yelled at him. Then, luckily, he met an old man who knew the Nanai language. He questioned Chokcho and showed him where Lyan the Manchu lived.

When at last the little Nanai came to the place, he saw a beautiful house. The corners of the roof were turned up. Little silver bells were hanging from the corners and ringing. There were windows made of transparent paper. All kinds of trees grew around the house—cherry trees and apple trees. Gold-colored birds were sitting on the branches. Music was playing everywhere. Brooks flowed between the trees, babbling, as though talking softly to each other.

Chokcho entered the house and shouted, "Hey, Lyan, come out and fight!" He had a stick ready, so as to fight Lyan to the death.

Nobody answered the little Nanai. It looked as though the man was not at home.

Chokcho entered Lyan's room. He put the acorn into the ashes in the hearth, so that it would lie on something soft for a while. He placed the pike

in the water in Lyan's washbasin. He stood the spit near the stove. He left the brake and the paddle at the door. Then he sat down on the bunk and fell asleep.

In the evening Lyan returned home. He was merry and drunk.

He started building a fire in the hearth. He bent over the fire and began blowing on the coals. Then the acorn jumped up and hit Lyan right in the eye! Lyan howled with pain and ran to the water basin to wash out his eye. Then the pike reached out of the basin and grabbed him by the nose. Lyan sprang away from the basin. Then the spit stabbed him in the back. Lyan became terribly frightened. He dashed toward the door and tried to run out. Then the brake and the paddle went at him. They beat him, pressed him, and squeezed him, so that he began to see stars! The brake and the paddle kept working him over until they had reduced him to a large, fine pelt.

Chokcho woke up and asked, "Did Lyan come home?"

His friends answered him, "He came to his misfortune! Look at what he has now become!"

Chokcho looked. He saw a soft, white pelt, just like leather, lying on the ground. Chokcho thanked his friends; he was only sorry that he had not settled with Lyan himself.

Chokcho found Beldy's furs in Lyan's house. He took the hunting supplies and all kinds of goods that Lyan had taken from people by cheating, and he put everything into Lyan's pelt. He collected his friends—the brake and the paddle, the acorn, the pike, and the spit. He stepped onto his marvelous skis.

The skis rose into the air again and flew like an arrow. They flew right under the noses of Lyan's servants.

The skis came to rest on the spot where Chokcho had found them. He left them there. "Thanks for your help. I don't want to take what belongs to someone else."

He placed the pike in the cool depths of the stream. He left the brake and the paddle at the abandoned fishing spot—they would come in handy for their master if he returned. He lay the spit down in its old place near the campfire. He threw the acorn into soft earth, so that it would sprout and a new tree would grow out of it.

And then Chokcho went on his way.

He came home rich. When he opened Lyan's pelt, everyone in the village was astonished at how much was crammed into it!

His mother and his sisters were happy that Chokcho had come back. They kissed him and hugged him and wouldn't let him out of their sight.

And then Chokcho spoke as a man and a hunter. He said, "My boots are all worn. Sew me some new ones. Tomorrow I will go to the taiga."

His sisters sewed him boots out of Lyan's pelt.

Those boots lasted a long time, because there is no skin tougher than the skin of a cheat and a thief who will not be moved to pity and will not be touched by the tears of those he has hurt.

Mambu the Orphan

The Ulch people have lived on the Amur for a long, long time. Since they first came here, little hills have become big, and big rivers have become small.

The three Ulch clans—the Sulaki, the Punadi, and the Gubatu—were related. They lived near each other: their villages stood alongside each other on the Amur shore.

The Ulches lived in harmony. All the people in the village built their houses together: some kneaded the clay, some hewed the posts, some carried the poles up to the roof. All the people in the village fished together: some went in a big boat, some went in a small boat, and some, sitting on a log, drove the fish into nets. They lived in friendship with the forest people and the river people. The Ulches always had seal and salmon and sable and elk.

In the Sulaki clan lived a boy named Mambu.

When Mambu was born, his mother washed him with her own milk for fifteen days. His father hung a little ax and a little knife above his cradle so that he would grow accustomed to weapons.

As soon as Mambu saw the knife, he grabbed it with both his hands and climbed out of his cradle.

His father and mother were astonished. "Our Mambu will be either a bogatyr or an unfortunate!" they thought to themselves.

Mambu stepped out of the house, threw a stone into an alder grove, and killed a grouse. He hung the bird over the door of his house so that everyone would see that a hunter had been born there.

"He will be the best among good people!" the villagers then said about Mambu.

Until that time the Sulakis had never seen any bad people. But soon they would have occasion to meet some.

In the fall, when the fish were running, the Sulakis stuffed their storehouses full of fish: dried fish for the dogs, sturgeon and salmon bellies, enough dried and cured fish for the whole winter. They gathered and stored lingonberries, wild strawberries, day-lily roots, and blueberries.

One day the Sulakis looked and saw a boat sailing on the Amur. It was a big boat; its bow and stern were upturned. The Ulches had never seen such a boat before. The boat had yellow sails, and a banner with a golden dragon was waving from the mast. Waves were playing in the boat's wake. Many people were sitting in the boat. In their hands they held swords two palms wide; in their hands they held spears twice as long as a man's height. Their foreheads were shaved; braids tied with black ribbons hung from the backs of their heads down to the floor.

The old men said, "We have to welcome these people. They are strangers, they must be from far away. They must have much news."

Mambu said, "These are bad people! We should flee from them into the taiga. Why are they holding swords in their hands? Why are they pointing their spears at us?"

The boat stopped at the Sulaki village. The people came out of the boat, carrying their chief on a litter. Eight carriers bent under his weight. On his head was a hat with a peacock feather and a ball of jasper. His robe was iridescent, shimmering with all the colors of the rainbow. The stranger had such a big belly that his face could not be seen over it.

Mambu looked at him and said, "This is not a man but a belly. He has come for no good."

"You don't understand anything!" the old men said.

The Ulches ran up to the strangers. Tribal law commanded that a stranger must be made warm and must be fed; he must be given the best pieces of food. The women brought fish, cereal, and all kinds of food on platters.

The man-belly, staring at the Ulches, said, "We are the Chinese king's people. Our king is the greatest king on the earth; in the whole world there is no one greater than our king! He has sent us to collect tribute from you."

The Ulches did not understand what tribute was. They had never paid tribute to anyone. They asked what it was.

The Chinese man-belly answered, "We will take one sable from you for each man in your village. We will do this every year, now and forever! In exchange, the Chinese king promises to grace you with his benevolence and to bestow favors on you. He will allow you to catch fish in the river, hunt animals in the forest, and breathe the air."

The people were astonished.

The women said, "These people must be poor. They probably don't have any sables. The Chinese king must be cold. Let him warm himself up— but not with our sables!"

But the Chinese people had already started going from house to house themselves. They went into all the houses, they entered all the storehouses, for the Ulches had no locks—against whom should they lock up, when they were among their own people? The Chinese warriors ransacked all the houses, dragging out the furs. They had long since taken a sable for each man, but they continued carrying out furs—bear and more sable and lynx and seal and fox and polecat—and putting them into their boat. They stared hard and breathed heavily as they grabbed the pelts—sometimes two of them grabbed the same pelt.

Mambu said to the man-belly, "Honorable man, your warriors have long since taken what you call tribute, and they are still carrying out our furs. Tell me, isn't it time to stop?"

The man-belly stirred. He raised his head. He looked at Mambu with eyes like those of the serpent Khimu. His eyes were burning with a green flame as though he would eat the boy!

"My warriors are taking the rest of the furs for me and for themselves for having brought the Chinese majesty's benevolence to you. We spent our own money and strength on the road: it took us a long time to get to you here."

The old men saw that because of the Chinese king's benevolence all their goods were gone. They shook their heads. They felt deeply hurt.

Mambu said, "We should take everything back from them!"

But how to take it back?

The Chinese people had put all the furs into their boat. The man-belly sat on top of them. Then they pushed off with their boathooks and started back.

Some guests! They didn't even look at the food; they only ravaged the storehouses. The women began to cry. The men started to swear.

Mambu got really angry. "If not for us, then not for them either!" he said.

He went to the riverbank and started to whistle.

Everyone knows that if you whistle next to the water, the wind will rise up. Mambu puffed up his cheeks. He took in so much air that all of him became round. He whistled for a long time. In answer to his whistling a small wind came running. The grass began to stir, the water on the river began to ripple, and the banner on the mast of the Chinese boat began to wave. Mambu kept on whistling. A middle-sized wind came flying to help his younger brother. Leaves on branches began to rustle, branches began to sway. Whitecaps began to dance on the waves in the river. The mast of the Chinese boat began to bend. And Mambu kept on whistling. The middle-sized wind saw he didn't have enough strength either, so he called to his older brother for help. The big wind came rushing. Trees began to bend and break. On the Amur the water became dark and the waves began to seethe, rising higher than the houses. On the Chinese boat the sails were torn off; on the Chinese boat the mast broke; the boat began to fill with water. And the wind was getting stronger and stronger!

It overturned the boat. The Chinese warriors fell into the water. The more heavily armed sank right to the bottom; those with fewer arms swam on the waves, swallowing water. And the man-belly rolled on the waves like a great balloon. He couldn't drown—he was so full of fat! All that the Chinese had taken from the Sulakis they lost in this storm, and they lost all their own things too. They barely managed to scramble out onto the opposite shore. They ran to the

Manchurian headman. He asked what they had taken from the Ulches for the Chinese king. The man-belly replied, squeezing the water out of his robe, "We took Amur water!"

And the wind kept getting stronger and stronger.

The Ulch houses began to sway. The poles on the roofs began to fall off. The old men told Mambu, "Stop blowing!" But Mambu had already let all the air out of his cheeks. The winds were already roaming on the Amur without him. Mambu shouted to them, "Enough!" But the winds were out of control—they did not hear him.

Then Mambu took his warrior's bow, pulled on the bowstring of elk sinew, put to the bow an arrow made of ironwood birch, attached a burning coal to the arrow, and shot it into the big wind. The big wind became frightened and ran home. And then the middle-sized wind and the small wind ran away too. It became very quiet. The waves calmed down. The trees stood straight again.

Mambu said, "The lynx always goes to the same watering place to drink. The Chinese people will come here again! We must leave this place. The man-belly will keep coming here until he eats us all up."

The old men did not listen. They did not want to leave their native place. "How could we?" they asked. "Our fathers are buried here."

Time passed. In the winter the Chinese people came to the Sulaki village again. They came on big sleds. Fearsome animals were harnessed to their sleds. Their heads were like those of reindeer, they had hair on their tails, round hooves on their four legs, and the hair on their necks fell to one side. Twice as many men came as before. And the man-belly was with them.

Again they demanded tribute. Again they went through the storehouses.

Mambu said to the man-belly, "Nobody has ever cut two branches from the same spot on a tree!"

The Chinese man shouted at Mambu and stamped his feet. Warriors rushed at Mambu, pushing him away.

Mambu went home. He got some bear fat, cut it up into pieces, and stole up to the Chinese sleds with it. He tied pieces of fat to the undersides of the sleds.

Again the Chinese cleaned out all of the Sulaki storehouses. They took furs, food, and all kinds of things. They got into their sleds. They shouted at their animals, and the animals galloped off. All you could hear was the runners squeaking, and all you could see was the snow whirling behind the sleds.

Again the women cried. The old men swore.

Mambu said to them, "Bring all the dogs here!"

They brought all the dogs that were in the village. Mambu took the strongest of the leaders, gave him a piece of bear fat to smell, and stuck his nose into the tracks of the Chinese sleds. The leader smelled the direction the fat had gone and dashed along its track. All the other dogs ran after him!

The man-belly was riding in his sled. He was happy that he had taken so much from the Ulches. How much he would give to the Chinese king, he did not count, and how much he would keep for himself, he did not say. The man-belly and his people had already reached the middle of the frozen Amur.

Then the dogs caught up with them.

The dogs could smell the bear fat, but they couldn't understand where the smell was coming from, so they threw themselves upon the Chinese people! They bit half of them to death; they scattered all the tribute on the snow. They bit the animals that the Chinese had harnessed to their sleds. The whole sled-train fell apart.

The Chinese started running, but the dogs hung onto them, and sank their teeth deeply into them. Somehow, after getting to the opposite shore, the man-belly managed to beat off the dogs.

The Chinese people came running to the Manchurian headman.

He asked them how much tribute they had taken from the Ulches, but to himself he was counting how much to send to the Chinese king and what to keep for himself.

The man-belly answered, pulling dogs' teeth out of his robe and his body, "Here, you see, we took dogs' teeth."

The headman became enraged. He commanded an army to be sent against the Sulakis. He ordered that they all be destroyed.

A whole storm cloud of Chinese went against the Ulches.

To their misfortune, Mambu was not in the village then. He had gone to visit the taiga people and had been delayed. He came home only the following summer.

He found that all the Sulakis had been killed and all their houses had been burned. There was not a single living soul in the whole village. Only the ravens crowed, and the hawks circled over the village in the sky. Mambu saw

that the Sulakis had fought bravely, had killed many Chinese warriors, but they had taken up arms too late and had all been slain.

Mambu the orphan began to cry.

But there was nothing to be done. You have to "raise your kinsmen's bones"—this is what the tribal law commands; you must avenge the dead! You must kill one enemy for each one dead. And he could not manage this all alone.

Mambu went to the Punadi clan to ask for help. He came to their village, but the ashes were already cold there. The Chinese had burned all the houses and carried off all the Punadis as prisoners.

Mambu went to the Gubatu clan to ask for help, to avenge the two clans. He came to their village. But the houses were standing empty there. The wind had covered everything with dust. Only rats were running around the village. The Gubatus had left their native village; they were afraid of the Chinese. Where they went, who knows? They left no tracks.

Mambu began to cry. How was he to bring vengeance on the enemy?

Mambu went to the river people to ask for help. The river people assembled. They heard Mambu out. An old kaluga man said to him, "The Sulakis and the Punadis were good people! We would be glad to help you, but we cannot live without water. How can we fight on dry land? We can't walk on land!"

Mambu went to the taiga people. They assembled, having learned that a human being had come to them, asking for help.

The taiga people became angry with the Chinese and began to roar. An old bear man said to Mambu the orphan that the taiga people would be glad to avenge the Sulakis, to avenge the Punadis—they were good people—but the taiga people could not swim across the river.

Mambu went to the forest people. He bowed to the birch tree and told it what misfortune had happened to him.

He said, "You can swim across a river, you can walk on dry land. I ask you to help me! Alone I cannot avenge my people."

The forest people agreed.

Mambu took an ax. He chopped down a great many birch trees. He peeled off the bark. He cut the wood into logs. He carved eyes on the logs so that they could see the road. He carved noses on the logs so that they could smell the smoke on the robes of those who had killed the Sulakis and carried away the Punadis. He slapped them with his hand. The logs moved their eyes and looked at Mambu. What was he going to say?

"You, wood people," said Mambu, "go to war! I cannot avenge every-one by myself! I ask you! I beg you—go! Don't leave a single enemy alive!"

He showed the wood people the road. They rolled into the river and swam in the direction from which the Chinese people had come.

Mambu sat down on the riverbank.

He neither ate nor drank, waiting for the wood people.

The wood people swam across the river. They galloped along the Chinese earth. They galloped up to the Chinese city. In the city the man-belly and the headman were sitting in the palace, dividing the rich booty and boasting about the blood they had spilled. And their warriors were also there—dividing the Ulches' possessions and quarreling over each pelt.

Suddenly the wood people came rushing through the windows and the doors and started beating the Chinese! The wood people were not afraid of swords. They did not listen to the shouts—they had no ears. You could not trip them—they had no feet. You could not beg for mercy—they had no hearts!

The wood people beat up all the Chinese. They beat the man-belly from both sides so hard that all that remained of him was a greasy spot on the floor. They gave the headman so many bumps that he could not recognize him-self for the rest of his life.

Mambu the orphan was sitting and waiting. He had become as black as earth.

The wood people returned. They climbed out on the shore.

"We gave beatings to all of them," they said. "What should we do next?"

"Thank you," Mambu said.

Then he closed the wood-people's eyes and hewed off their noses. They became plain logs again. Mambu chopped down some willow branches, tied the logs with them, and made a raft. He got on the raft and pushed himself off with a pole, away from his native shore. Then he started to cry. "How could I live here alone? A man cannot live by himself. I will float down the Amur to look for other people. I will forget my name. I will ask to be taken into a strange clan."

Mambu floated down the Amur.

He will float on the river as long as he has the strength. He will float past a village and will shout, "Hey, people, take me as one of your own! Give me a name! Accept me into your clan!"

But Mambu will not float for long.

Any village would take such a young man. Any old man would call such a young man his son; all Mambu has to do is call out.

But of the Sulakis, the Punadis, and the Gubatus nothing has been heard since that time. Only old men tell of them in their tales.

How the Beldys Stopped Fighting

Of all the Nanai, the Beldys were the bravest. They were also said to be the most quarrelsome. Fighting was the most important thing in the world to them. How many times they had made war on their neighbors! They could never stop fighting.

Woe to anyone who killed a Beldy! Blood vengeance! The killing could not go unavenged! But while in other clans only a brother, son, or the father would avenge the victim, among the Beldys the whole clan would go on the march. And there were many Beldys. Instead of killing one enemy, they would kill several. Then those they had fought against would come back for revenge.

And so it went. The Beldys were always either on the march or under siege.

It got so that they had no time for hunting, no time for fishing. All they had was war and more war!

Beldy boys grasped a warrior's bow of honeysuckle wood in their cradles.

The girls, from early childhood, whenever they heard a noise in the road, climbed under the bunks and hid there.

And nobody could do anything with these Nanai: "We are of the tiger clan," they liked to say.

The Beldys were so accustomed to war that when there was no fighting they walked around feeling lost, not knowing what to do with themselves.

One day twins were born to a Nanai of the Beldy clan. Everyone in the clan rejoiced, because they knew that if one member of a clan has twins, the whole clan will have great luck. That is what the old men said. They also said that twins must be honored. And so all the Beldys honored the twins and took care of them. They gave them good names: they called one Udoga and the other Chubak.

The Beldys honored their twins and often sought their advice. And as for the women, they, of course, did too. It sometimes happened that the young twins were the only men left in the village. They were still so little they didn't go to war—they sat on the bunk in the house and played with little knives. But the twins were wise: they knew everything.

Whenever anything happened, the women went to them to ask what to do.

A woman would come running to Udoga and Chubak, saying she had dreamed of a cuckoo crying.

The twins would ask, "What kind of a voice did the cuckoo have?"

"A hoarse voice," the woman would answer.

"That's a sign of death," Udoga would say.

Then the women would start crying.

Time would pass, and the Beldys would return from war, and, sure enough, they would be dragging the dead on mats behind them.

In the spring the women would come to the twins and ask, "How will the fish run this year?"

Chubak would say, "Bring me a migrating bird."

They would bring it. Chubak would look at it. "The bird is fat," he would say. "There will be a great deal of fish."

In winter they would ask Udoga and Chubak, "Where should we place our fishing tents, on high ground or on low?"

"The moon is low in the sky this winter," Chubak would answer. "Set the fishing spot up on high ground—the water will be high."

This is how the twins lived. They were growing up, little by little.

Once, no sooner did the Beldys return from a campaign than there was trouble again. Someone in the Zaksuli clan had taken a weasel out of one of their traps!

The Beldys raised a great uproar and began to bustle about, to prepare spears, sharpen knives, and make arrows. The women ran to the twins; they cried and shouted that it wasn't worth going to war over a weasel. As it was, there were fewer men in the village each year.

And the men also came to seek advice from the twins.

Chubak told them, taking his warrior's bow in his hands, "This is a great insult! If someone had taken a sable out of our trap, we could forgive him. A sable is worth a great deal of money. With that money a man could buy food, with that money a man could buy clothing. Therefore it must have been need that made him take that sable. And how could we not help a poor man? But a weasel is a worthless animal. You can buy neither clothing nor food for the price of its pelt, so someone took it out of mischief. The people who took it don't consider us to be men. They think we cannot stand up for ourselves! They took a trifle—that means they look on us as dead; it is just as if they really killed us. We must fight!"

Udoga said, taking his spear in his hands, "We have to fight the Zaksulis! We have to kill all the Zaksulis! The Zaksulis are bad people—they stole a weasel from us. But when we go to war against them, we must take an oath: to take no food or water from their earth."

The women were sad; they saw that even the twins wanted to fight, so there was nothing they could do. They prepared food for the men: they baked cakes, and they dried fish; they gave them day-lily roots and cured meat.

And so the Beldys went off to war.

They loaded sacks of food on their backs, they tied pitchers of water around their necks. They walked, and as they walked they panted. Their loads were heavy! The farther they went, the angrier they became. What wicked people these Zaksulis were! It wasn't bad enough that the Beldys were obliged to wage war against them, but they had to carry such heavy supplies, too.

They crossed three rivers, they crossed nine lakes.

They saw some women from the Zaksuli clan picking lingonberries. Chubak called to them.

"Go to the village and tell the men," he said, "we will kill all your people, we won't leave a single person alive!"

Now the Beldys became frightened. "Why did you tell them that? Now they will know we are coming. How can we go after them weighed down with pitchers and sacks?"

Chubak did not answer. He did not say anything.

The women ran to the village. They told their husbands, they told their brothers. The men went into their houses. Where else could they hide from the Beldys! They sat indoors and did not show themselves. The Beldys drew close to the village. They laid siege to the village, hiding in the tall grass and in the shrubs. They watched for the Zaksulis and waited.

And the women of the village walked all around, poking in the grass and the shrubs with clubs. They were going to club one Beldy after another, so hard that they would see stars.

The Beldys kept quiet and endured patiently. They moved farther away from the women so as not to get angry at them. You must not touch women.

The Zaksuli men sat in their houses. They were terribly afraid.

The Beldys sat in the bushes, watching for the enemy. They didn't let them catch fish, they didn't let them hunt birds.

As long as they had food and water, the Beldys were very brave.

But then they ran out of food. Still the Beldys sat, enduring patiently.

Chubak said, "Now we have to wait only a little longer! The Zaksulis will soon die of fright."

Then the Beldys ran out of water. They still endured patiently, not saying anything.

Udoga said, "Now we have to wait only a very little more!"

Then the Beldys ran out of patience. They sat grumbling at this kind of war; they were getting thin; they were growing so weak their spears were dropping out of their hands.

And it was no easier for the Zaksulis, sitting locked up in their houses, hungry. They sat and sat, until they could bear it no longer. Then they sent an old man to the Beldys. He took with him a stick with a human face. He set out, staggering in the wind.

And the Beldys were no better off—they had become as thin as a bear

in spring. The old man begged for peace. They began to discuss their differences. The twins said to the esteemed old man, "You are very guilty before us. We will take a large fine from you for that. No one has ever had to pay such a large fine before!"

The old man became frightened and started to shake. How would the Zaksulis ever pay a big fine? The Zaksulis were very poor people.

Chubak said, "Ay, what a big fine! A pot, a spear—and a kerchief to wipe off the shame."

The Beldys opened their eyes wide and started to tremble. Some large fine!

Was that worth enduring hunger and thirst for?

Was that worth going to war for?

In their minds was but one thought: to get home as fast as possible, to eat and to drink to their hearts' content!

The Zaksulis were happy. They paid the fine at once.

In addition, they gave Udoga and Chubak beautiful girls for wives, in order to become related to the Beldys and never have to quarrel again.

The Beldys took the girls. They ran home. Where had their strength come from?

When they were home, the women asked them, "How was the war?"

The Beldys said, "Ay, what a war it was! The most terrible war—there has been no worse!"

The Beldys began to drink water. They drank for three days. They drank up a whole lake. They drank it all up, so that the lake has been dry ever since. The Beldys began to eat. They ate for three days. They ate everything up, even their elkskin robes.

From that time on they have never fought with their kinsmen. They have settled all their differences in peace.

Thanks to Udoga and Chubak, who taught them some sense!

The Twins

This happened not so long ago, and there are some old men still living who remember it—although it's true that there are only a few of these old men left.

In the Beldy clan there lived twin boys called Udoga and Chubak. It is well known that it's a very good sign when twins are born, for twins bring great luck to the whole clan. Udoga and Chubak lived the way all children do. They were not very big, yet their minds caught up quickly with those of the old men. Only five winters had passed since their birth, but Udoga and Chubak already went hunting. And they always had luck. Both the taiga people and the river people loved the twins, so they would help the brothers in every way, sending them good luck in all they did.

Once a bad year came: animals were scarce, and the fish ran poorly. The old men began to say that the clan should move to another place, that in this place demons had frightened the animals and the fish away.

Udoga heard the old men out and asked, "What's wrong with this place?"

He pulled the bowstring of his little bow, looked around, and sent his arrow flying off into the taiga. Whether it flew for a long time, I do not know, but then it returned and went right back into its place in Udoga's quiver. And birds came flying behind the arrow—ducks, geese, quail—and they all lay down at Udoga's feet. The old men saw that every bird had been hit in the left eye. The men grinned at one another. "If this happens every time, the village will not be without meat!"

Then Chubak asked the old men, "What's wrong with this place?"

He threw his net into the water with one hand. The net sank.

"Well," thought the old men, "the water demon has carried the net away."

They waited a while. Suddenly the river seethed and boiled and foamed with bubbles. Then Chubak thrust his hand into the water, grabbed the net, and pulled it in. Chubak pulled in as many fish as there were knots in the net. The old men stared at one another. "Eh, if this happens every time, the village will not be without fish!"

Then Chubak asked the women, "Last year, on which side did the salmon have more roe?"

"On the left," they answered.

"That means that this year the fish are running near the left bank," said Chubak. "You have to study the signs. You were fishing near the right bank, so it looked to you as though there were no fish, as though the fish had disappeared."

Then also Udoga spoke. "The birds and the animals go after the fish. So you should have hunted also on the other bank."

From then on the old men started asking the twins' advice about everything. And all went well.

Only soon another misfortune came! From a faraway shore came a

Manchu headman sailing up the Amur. He came with sampans filled with soldiers and cannons. He demanded tribute from the Beldys—from each man a sable, an otter, and a fox.

The Beldys grew downhearted. They had never paid tribute to anyone, and now, suddenly—but there was nothing else to be done. The pigtailed Manchu had power! He had twice as many soliders as there were Beldys.

The old men went to the twins and asked for their advice. Udoga and Chubak looked at each other. At last Udoga said, "Don't pay any tribute. We are not Manchurian people. We are people of Amur land and water! My brother and I will go to the headman."

The village women start to cry.

"You mustn't go!" they wailed. "The Manchu headman is bad! He will kill our twins—he will destroy our good luck!"

But Udoga and Chubak went to the headman anyway. The headman was sitting in his big painted sampan, on a wide platform, under a fluttering silk tent. Guards stood all around. An executioner was sharpening a curved sword next to his block. The headman rested his right hand on a cushion. His fingernails were so very, very long they reached the floor. They were bent and twisted, and each was fitted into a long silver case. Five slave girls were cleaning the headman's nails. A fat scribe sat at the headman's feet holding a big book.

When the headman saw the twins, he said, "What do Nanai children want here?"

The scribe bent down to the ground before the headman. "These children have come to say, honorable headman, that the old Nanai men will come soon to bring you the tribute you ordered to be taken from them."

The headman looked even more imperious. He turned up his nose. He looked at the blue sky so as not to have to look at the old Nanai men and ruin his eyes. He waited and waited until his neck began to hurt, but still the old Nanai men didn't come.

Then Chubak said, "The old men will not come, honorable headman! The Beldys have never paid tribute to anyone. They have caught fish in their own rivers, hunted animals in their own taiga, walked on their own earth, and breathed their own air. They laugh at the idea of paying tribute. They would laugh if they came to pay. And so, in order not to hurt your feelings, they do not come at all. But we are only little boys; we don't understand anything. Here, headman, we have brought you some presents."

Udoga poured a pinch of Amur earth out of a tobacco pouch.

"Headman, accept a pinch of our earth if your own is not enough for you."

Chubak took an owl's eye out of a birchbark bowl.

"Headman, accept my present, too—an owl's eye. Then you will be able to see, even at night, that brave people live on the Amur."

Udoga pulled a feather from the tail of a red-beaked eagle.

"Headman, accept my wish that you live as many years as an eagle and that everyone be as afraid of you as of an eagle. But on the Amur there will be no fear of you!"

Chubak poured a pinch of ashes out of a birchbark bowl.

"Let all your enemies turn to ashes, headman! Let all evil thoughts against the Amur people be buried in ashes!"

The headman was astonished at the way the little Nanai spoke. He became frightened; if this is what their children were like, then what were the Nanai warriors and men like? But he didn't show that he was afraid. He hid his fear and shouted at the twins, "Tomorrow I will send my soldiers to the Beldys! I will burn all those who are already dead and kill all those who are alive!"

Udoga bowed to him. "As you wish, honorable headman, but tomorrow you will have no success. You had better do today what you said you would do."

The headman did not listen. He waited until the next day and then made ready to march. But it began to rain so hard that the riverbanks disappeared from sight, and all the roads were washed out. The headman's soldiers set off, but they nearly drowned in the mud. The powder in their guns became damp. There was nothing for the soldiers to do but march back.

"The sun set into a storm cloud yesterday," Udoga said. "That was a sign of heavy rain. A sure sign!"

The bad weather passed. The sky became studded with stars.

The headman said, "Tomorrow I will sail to the Beldys' villages. I will destroy everybody! I will kill all those who are alive; I will burn all the houses to ashes!"

"As you wish, honorable headman," said Chubak, "but tomorrow you will have no success. You had better do today what you said you would do."

The headman waited for the next day. In the morning he ordered the sails to be raised on all the sampans so they could sail to the Beldys' villages.

From the west a black cloud, circled with a white ring, swooped down—

and a storm came up such as the headman had never seen in his whole life! The Amur began to surge. Waves rose up to the sky; clouds came down to the ground. The wind blew once—it tore all the sails on the sampans. The wind blew a second time—it broke all the oars and masts. The sampans were scarcely left in one piece. It was lucky the wind did not blow a third time.

Chubak said, "Yesterday the stars twinkled brightly; that was a sign of a storm."

The headman sat there, very angry. He covered his head with his robe; he didn't want to look at anyone; he wouldn't let anyone near him. He broke all his nails in his rage. He chased away all his slave girls. He beat his scribe with a club.

The twins approached him. They said, "Until now, we have told you things, honorable headman. Now you tell us something. You have seen that we know our land and that we rightly collect our tribute from it: we take fish, furs, and fowl. But how do you expect to collect tribute from a land that you do not know?"

The headman turned pale. He thought, "How will I manage to deal with a people whose very children are wise beyond belief?"

The Manchu headman sailed away, back to his own shore.

This happened not so very long ago. Some old men are still alive who remember the twins. Or maybe they heard about Udoga and Chubak from their fathers. Who knows?

The Golden Neckband

When a man is stupid, it is bad; but when he is both stupid and greedy—it is twice as bad! A stupid and greedy man will never do any good, either for himself or for others.

In a village there lived a shaman named Chumboka.

There were many children in that village. They liked to wrestle, to run races, to play tug-of-war.

They were good children and clever! All the fathers loved their children.

The shaman Chumboka had a son named Akimka. The shaman was rich. He lived by fraud: he said that he possessed much knowledge; he said that he was allied with demons—he could bewitch or cure any man. When anyone in the village was sick, the shaman was called. Chumboka would come, look at the sick one, and say, "A demon has gotten into him! I know this demon; I know who he is. He must be expelled."

He would tighten the skin of his tambour and begin to beat it; he would make a fire and circle around and around it. He would say some words, as though he were talking to the demons, asking them to go away and leave the sick man alone, and threatening them if they didn't. If the sick man got well, the shaman would say, "See, I drove away the demons. I am powerful! Bring me your gifts." If the sick man died, the shaman would say, "The gifts weren't big enough; the people didn't believe in me enough. That's why the demons carried the sick man away."

The villagers were afraid of the shaman. They brought him all kinds of gifts. Some of them denied themselves things in order to bring gifts to Chumboka.

Chumboka grew very, very rich. Chumboka grew proud. He walked around the village—so big, so full of fat that his robe became greasy through and through. Chumboka turned up his nose—he thought he was better than anyone else.

The shaman's son Akimka was like all the children—no better, no worse.

The shaman was annoyed that his son was just like everyone else's. He decided to do something to make him different from all the other children. He went to the smith with a piece of gold.

"Listen, smith, make me a golden neckband."

"What do you need a neckband for, and a golden one at that?" the smith asked the shaman.

"I will put it around my son's neck," said the shaman. "It will distinguish Akimka and let everybody see what a rich father he has!"

The smith said, "It's not nice, Chumboka, to set your son off from the other children."

The shaman became angry. "You're stupid!" he said. "You're stupid, and yet you're giving me advice!"

"I'm not stupid!" The smith's feelings were hurt.

"If you're not stupid," said Chumboka, "then guess this riddle. What is this: white people who chop and a red man who carries away."

The smith thought and thought, but he couldn't guess.

Chumboka started to laugh at him. "Eh, you! The answer is teeth and tongue. You couldn't even guess a simple riddle!"

The smith didn't say anything. He made the golden neckband and gave it to the shaman.

Chumboka went home. He put the band around his son's neck and told him not to play with the other children.

Akimka walked around the village all by himself. The band shone on his neck. Chumboka was happy. Now everybody could see that Akimka's father wasn't just a common person.

And time passed.

Akimka grew. He had stopped playing children's games; he became too lazy to run. He got fat. The golden band became tight—it began to pinch his neck. Akimka complained, "Father, take off the neckband!"

Chumboka took hold of the band—he turned it and twisted it, but he couldn't take it off. Akimka had grown too big; he was panting and gasping for breath.

The mother said to Chumboka, "Break the band, Chumboka!"

Chumboka became frightened.

"Why, how could I do that!" he said. "The golden band is expensive. If you break it, you'll ruin the thing! Akimka is gasping because there are too many common people here—the air is bad. Let Akimka sit on a hillock for a while."

Akimka sat on a hillock, wheezing.

Chumboka was almost crying himself—he was so sorry for his son. But he would have been even sorrier to see the golden band ruined.

Then the smith came to the shaman and said, "Well, which of us is stupid now?"

"You—you are stupid!" Chumboka shouted.

"Well, if you're so smart, guess this riddle. What is this: a pot without a bottom."

The shaman thought a while.

"Eh," he said, "you call that a riddle? A pot without a bottom is a hole in the ice on the river."

The smith said to him, "No, you didn't guess it right, Chumboka! A pot without a bottom is your greed. No matter how much you throw into it, the pot still stays empty. Saw the band apart!"

"Why!" the shaman shouted. "You'll ruin the thing!"

The smith spit into Chumboka's eyes and left.

And, after all that, the shaman's son Akimka died with the golden band around his neck. Even the pure air didn't help him.

When Chumboka saw his dead son, he began to howl. But it was too late—he could never bring Akimka back.

Kile Bamba and the Loche Bogatyr

This probably happened not too long ago. There lived a man named Kile Bamba on the Amur River—Kile Bamba, a man of the Nanai people, Kile Bamba, a man of bogatyr strength.

Kile Bamba was born of an ordinary woman. But good spirits must have been helping him, because he grew up very fast. He was still sucking on a pacifier when he had his first encounter with an animal. One day his mother had gone out. She had leaned a log against the house door so that it would stay closed. How much time she spent visiting the neighbors I do not know, but while she was out a tiger jumped into Bamba's house through an open window.

The neighbors heard the tiger's roar. Then they heard little Bamba crying. The kinsmen scattered in all directions. How could they not run, with a tiger in the village!

Bamba cried for a while; then he stopped.

"Well," the kinsmen thought, "little Bamba has perished; the tiger has carried him off into the taiga!"

His mother came running home.

Bamba was lying on his back, blowing bubbles out of his nose, playing with the tiger's striped tail. The tiger lay next to the cradle—little Bamba had strangled him. That's what Bamba did!

When he saw his mother, he took the pacifier out of his mouth. "What a bother," he said. "There are so many animals around now! They jump into windows; they don't let me sleep! I'll have to go after them myself," he said, "since there aren't any men in the village!"

Bamba stood up. He picked up his father's spear and tried it out for size.

"It's a little too small!" he said. He took the spear in both hands, pressed down on it, and broke it in two. "It's not very strong," he said.

Then he went into the taiga. He took hold of a young larch with his left hand. He twisted it and pulled it out with its roots, stripped off the branches, shook the earth off the roots, and tried it out to see how it felt.

"It's a little too light," he said. "But since there is nothing else, what can I do? I'll have to use this one."

His kinsmen looked at him in wonder: whom did he take after? There had never been a Nanai like this before. And they began to call him not Kile Bamba but Mergen Bamba—Bamba the bogatyr.

Bamba became so great a hunter that there was none better. Bamba would no sooner come out of the house and start getting ready to hunt than animals beyond nine hills, beyond nine lakes, would wake up in their lairs and start saying good-bye to their young ones—they knew they couldn't get away from Bamba!

Bamba had a sharp eye: he could take one quick look and tell immediately how many silver hairs there were on the fox's back and how many white ones in its tail. Bamba had a sharp ear: he could listen for one short moment and say, "Beyond nine rivers and nine streams baby sables are squealing. That's where the trap should be set."

Bamba had great strength: he could hunt animals for a hundred days without rest; then he'd sleep for only one night and hunt animals for another hundred days.

Bamba ate a great deal. He'd eat a mountain goat in the morning, an elk for dinner, and a bear for supper! He would pat his belly and say, "I could eat some more, but I must leave some food for tomorrow!"

When Bamba hunted with his kinsmen, only he would shoot the game; then ten hunters would collect it. When he returned from the hunt, a whole train of dog sleds came after him, carrying the furs. That's what Bamba was like!

Bamba was kind. If he heard a child crying anywhere in the village, he'd go to it and say, "Why are you crying? Here's a fish bladder for you. Play with it." He would give a blown-up fish bladder to the child; the child would hit the bladder with the palm of his hand, listen to the sound, and stop crying.

Bamba killed so many bears that he hung a bear's tooth over the cradle of every child in the village, to bring good luck and keep evil spirits from frightening the children. Everybody in the village had enough to eat—there was ample meat, plenty of fish, and fur in abundance.

The Nanai went across the river to the Chinese kingdom to trade. They sold furs and bought robes and supplies. The Nanai had round faces, stout bellies, and clear eyes. Their braids were tied with red plaits; they wore beautiful goatskin boots embroidered with silk; their hands were skillful, their feet swift. That's what the Nanai were like.

The Chinese headman looked and looked at the Nanai who came from the other side of the river. He became envious. The Nanai lived well and harmoniously; they paid tribute to no one and had everything they needed. The headman had stripped his own Chinese peasants long ago: he took for himself, he took for the king, he took for the soldier, he took for the monk, he took for the merchant, and once more for himself; what, then, could be left for the peasant? The headman thought, "Let me take tribute from the Nanai! The tribute I take from them will make even more wealth for me."

He sent his soldiers and his officials to the Nanai. They went with swords, with spears, with firearms—an immense host.

When they arrived, the Nanai welcomed them as guests and offered them food. But the Chinese did not look at the food—they went into the storehouses. Bamba became angry with the Chinese.

"You are boors," he said. "You don't know how guests should behave!"

The Manchu headman's soldiers wore their hair in pigtails. Bamba grabbed them by their long pigtails, tied the soldiers' braids together, and threw them into the river. The Chinese bobbed around in the water for a while and then sank. Bamba was strong!

The Manchu headman sent his soldiers to the Nanai time after time—he never saw any of them again.

The headman then realized that he couldn't take the Amur people by force. He started thinking; he called all his wise men and officials together so they could help him figure out how to collect wealth from the Amur land. The Chinese wise men thought and thought, and at last they came up with an idea.

The oldest man said to the headman, "Don't send soldiers to the Nanai. A soldier thinks with his sword and not with his head. Send them a merchant. A merchant is like a spider: he will attach himself to his victim and will not tear himself away until he has drunk up all the blood!"

And that is what the headman did; he sent the merchant Li-Chan.

Li-Chan came to the Nanai on the Amur. He was like a fox—he spoke honeyed words, he promised them all sorts of things. Li-Chan talked a blue streak—his tongue wagged like a fox's tail in the wind. The merchant started giving the Nanai goods on credit. "Take it, take it; we'll settle accounts later!" To one he gave beads, to another a pot; another got a printed robe, and another got earrings; still another got grain and flour. "Take it, take it—we'll settle later!" The Nanai thought that Li-Chan was kind. The Nanai thought they could get along with this merchant. He didn't shout, didn't threaten, didn't stamp his feet; he did everything with a smile and kept chuckling.

Li-Chan did all these things so that the Nanai would become accustomed to him. They stopped going to the Chinese kingdom to trade; they stopped buying goods there; they bought whatever they needed from Li-Chan. The merchant had everything they asked for.

Then the time came to pay Li-Chan what they owed him.

The Nanai brought furs to Li-Chan.

But suddenly all of Li-Chan's things became very expensive. He said that it had been hard to bring in the goods—the road was difficult, there were robbers on the road; he had to pay the headman, he had to pay the robbers, he even had to pay the Chinese king.

The Nanai gave him all their furs, but the furs did not cover their debt. They still owed a lot to Li-Chan. Well, the kind of people the Nanai were—they had to pay their debts before they could do anything else! So the Nanai began working to pay off the debt. Whatever they caught in the taiga they took to Li-Chan. Whatever they caught in the river they also took to him. Li-Chan had come to the Nanai thin as a worm; now he became fat as a pig. But the Nanai were growing thinner and thinner. They just couldn't work off their debt.

They thought and thought, and they went to Kile Bamba.

"This is how things are," they sighed. "We just can't pay off our debt! The devil must have gotten himself mixed up in this. At first Li-Chan counted a pelt as one pelt. Then Li-Chan started counting two pelts as one pelt. Now Li-Chan counts three pelts as one pelt. What should we do?"

Bamba went to the merchant. He was angry and he asked, "How did this happen?" So Li-Chan showed him the book—all the debts were written down in it. Bamba looked, but he couldn't understand the marks in the book. He could see that something was really written down there, and if there were as many debts as marks, the Nanai would never get out of debt! The thought never even crossed Bamba's mind that there might be more fraud than debts in that book.

Bamba asked the Nanai what they had taken from Li-Chan. They all answered at once. "I took a robe"—"I took some grain"—"I took some vodka—but I don't remember any more after that!" What they took before the vodka, the Nanai remembered; what they took after it, they didn't—the vodka had knocked all memory out of the Nanai.

Bamba decided to help his kinsmen.

But he didn't get his kinsmen out of trouble; instead he also got himself into trouble—he too went into debt to Li-Chan. How this happened, Bamba never knew.

"Li-Chan must be a devil and not a merchant," Bamba thought. "I don't understand how he can make three pelts count as one."

Bamba went to the shaman to ask him about the merchant. But the shaman was sitting dead drunk; he was hardly able to move his thick tongue. He listened and listened to Bamba, and then he said, "You are right! Li-Chan must be a devil! Look at the vodka he gave me. I drank it three days ago, and I'm still drunk. Can an ordinary person do such a thing? Certainly this Li-Chan is a devil!"

"Well, and what can a hunter do against a devil?"

"Nothing!"

Bamba said to the shaman, "Make magic! Drive this devil Li-Chan away! The Nanai keep taking all their catch to him, and they keep getting thinner and thinner. Soon they'll start dying!"

The shaman answered, "I can't make magic against Li-Chan. I can't manage his kind of devil—a Chinese devil, not a Nanai one. He is a devil's devil! Take more furs to him!"

"I will go into the dark forest to hunt animals," Bamba said. "I will go into the Sikhote Alin Mountains to get tiger, snow leopard, and lynx!"

"You can't go there. Hunt here," said the shaman. "Mountain devils live in the Sikhote Alin Mountains. The Udege mountain man Kakzamu guards those mountains; he turns people into stone!"

"I will go to the Big Sea! I'll get all kinds of seals," said Bamba.

The shaman waved both his hands at him. "Hunt here! The water devil Ganka lives in the Big Sea. He has a man's body, a fish's tail, and instead of a hand an iron hook that sticks out of the water. He grabs people with that hook!"

"I'll go into the swamps—I will get bittern, heron, and duck," said Bamba.

The shaman spit. "Hunt here, I tell you! The one-legged devil Boko lives in the swamp. He will lead you around in the swamp and drag you into the quagmire. Then you will lie in the quagmire and blow bubbles!"

"I will go to the treeless mountains," Bamba said then. "I will get elk and mountain goat!"

The shaman began to shake. "Hunt here, I tell you! Agdy—thunder— lives in the treeless mountains. He chops down trees with a stone ax. When he strikes, he turns a man into dust!"

"I will go to Lake Mylki; I will hunt beaver and geese!"

The shaman became so furious at Bamba that he began to foam at the mouth. "Khimu, the most terrible of all devils, lives in that lake! When he sees a man, he crawls out of the lake, and he burns the grass and the stones under him! Khimu will breathe fire on you—you will burn up, and no one will know!"

Kile Bamba lowered his head. He became thoughtful. What good was Bamba the bogatyr? There were devils all around. And all of them were stronger than the bogatyr. His bogatyr strength could not help him. Oy-ya-kha! Things were really bad.

"Hunt as you have hunted," said the shaman. "Take furs to Li-Chan. He will give you vodka—you'll forget all your troubles."

Bamba didn't want to go to Li-Chan. He went where his feet carried him.

He crossed three streams, he walked around six lakes, he climbed over nine hills. He picked out a spot; he built a tent and made a fire. He lay down in the tent. He began to think bitter thoughts.

"What good is a bogatyr's strength when the devils don't let him live? It isn't enough that there are devils in the forest, devils in the taiga, devils in the mountains, and devils in the river—now there is a Li-Chan in the village! Where can I find the strength to kill all those devils, so that people can live well again?"

Kile Bamba fell asleep. He slept, and in his sleep he heard someone coming from the direction of the Amur headwaters. Someone was walking with a heavy step, trampling the taiga under him and squeezing the water out of the ground. Bamba sprang up, put an arrow to his bow, and pulled out his knife. "Who goes there?"

Then a man came out from behind the trees. Bamba had never seen a man like him before. His face was white, his eyes were blue, his hair was as yellow as gold, and he had a thick beard. He was not dressed like a man from the Amur. He was holding an iron stick in his hands.

"One more devil has come!" thought Bamba.

But the man said to him, "What are you holding onto the bow for? Are you thinking of shooting at me? I am your friend, not your enemy. And why are you setting your bow against me, anyway? Let's have a contest—let's see who can shoot the farthest."

What bogatyr would refuse a contest!

Bamba put on a self-assured air. Nobody in the whole village could shoot farther than he! He saw a hare running beyond three streams. Bamba shot an arrow—he nailed the hare to a pine tree.

"Good!" said the man with yellow hair.

Then the man raised his stick.

"Beyond six streams," he said, "a squirrel is about to jump from one tree to another. I will kill it."

He aimed his stick, squinted one of his blue eyes. Something went crash-bang, like thunder roaring suddenly and re-echoing over the hills!

Kile Bamba became frightened and fell to the ground.

"Oy, Agdy—thunder," he said, "don't touch me!"

"That wasn't Agdy; that was I," the man laughed.

Bamba looked and saw that the squirrel was lying on its side already.

"You win," said Bamba. "Let's wrestle."

They took off their clothes, each took hold of the other's waist, and they started to wrestle. Neither could win. Neither could get the other down. Bamba tried to throw the man over his shoulder, but the man raised Bamba into the air and would not let him down. He kept holding him up there.

Everything went dark before Bamba's eyes. He said, "Let me down on the ground—I'm not a bird. I feel bad away from the ground. You win. Let's have a contest to see who can dance better."

Bamba started dancing. He began in the morning and kept dancing until the sun set. Nobody on the Amur had ever danced like that!

Then the man cleared his throat, spit on his palms, and started in his turn. He danced all night, he danced all day; a second night was coming, and he was still dancing. All you could hear was crashing and stamping along the valley. The water was splashing out of the river, the ground was shaking, the dust was rising in a cloud, hiding the stars.

"Hey, friend," shouted Bamba, "enough! You win!"

But the man kept dancing for three more days and nights, slapping his heels with his palms. Then he stopped and said, "That's not dancing! When I was young—did I dance then!"

"Would a bad man dance like that?" Bamba thought. "He has strong hands, a sharp eye, and a jolly disposition—why shouldn't we be friends?"

So they decided to become sworn brothers.

"I am Kile Bamba," said the Nanai.

"I am Ivan the Russian—'Loche' in your language."

"Are you a bogatyr in your land?" asked Bamba.

Loche waved his hand.

"What kind of a bogatyr am I?" he asked. "Bogatyrs will come after me; I am just my mother's youngest son."

"What did you come here for?" asked Bamba.

"I will live here. My fathers lived on this land a long time ago."

"It's bad here," said the Nanai.

"Why? Is the earth bad?" asked Ivan. He picked up a clump of earth, crumbled it in his hands, smelled it. "This earth is good!"

"There are so many devils," said Bamba, "they don't let us live!"

Bamba told Ivan about his troubles—how the devils had ensnared him hand and foot and taken his bogatyr strength away.

"Never mind," said Ivan, "just so long as we see the truth—the devils we'll take care of!"

Then they went to the village. The Nanai were walking around, looking very pale—they had nothing to eat. Only Li-Chan was sitting on the doorstep of his house—fat and red, like a tick.

"Is this one the devil?" asked Ivan.

"That's the one!"

Ivan and Bamba went into the storehouses. The storehouses were standing empty, with only cobwebs in the corners. Ivan collected the cobwebs and rolled them into a ball. Then he went to Li-Chan.

"Give me the book," he said. "Where does it say how much my friend Bamba owes you?"

Li-Chan got the book, opened it, and pointed at a page with his fat finger.

Ivan took the book and said, "If Bamba really owes you something—his word is so trustworthy that even fire will not destroy it! But if you have cheated Bamba, your word will burn up!"

He threw the book into the fire. Immediately the flames seized it and burned it up. Li-Chan shouted at Ivan and stamped his feet. Then Ivan took the ball of cobwebs that he had collected in the Nanai storehouses and hurled it into Li-Chan's mouth. At once Li-Chan grew thin, shrank, became small, and changed into a spider. Ivan threw him into the river, and Li-Chan floated to the Manchu headman who was his master.

The Nanai were still walking around feeling hungry.

Ivan took some small seeds out of his tunic and threw them onto the ground. Green grass began to grow out of the earth. It became yellow. Yellow seeds swelled in its stalks. Ivan took the seeds and ground them between two stones—the seeds turned to white dust. Ivan mixed the dust with Amur water—he made dough. He baked flat cakes out of the dough and gave them to the Nanai. "Eat!" he said.

The Nanai ate them. They tasted good! The food immediately made them stronger—much stronger than any food had ever done before.

The Nanai went hunting.

Bamba and Ivan also went hunting, together.

"I would like to get some elk," said Ivan. "Let's go to the treeless mountains!"

"Agdy—thunder—lives there," said Bamba.

Ivan wasn't frightened. And how can you fall behind your sworn brother—you will lose face! So Bamba went too. Ivan started firing out of his stick—he made such loud thunder that Agdy fled from those mountains.

"This is a good hunting spot," said Ivan. "So where is your Agdy?"

The sworn brothers went on. They walked into the swamp. Bamba saw a little hunchbacked, one-legged man standing in their way; his eyes were burning with a blue flame.

"Don't go farther, Ivan!" shouted Bamba. The hunchbacked devil—Boko—is standing there! He'll lead you into the quagmire and will destroy you!"

Ivan said, "Is this the evil Boko?" He seized Boko by his one leg and put him down under his own feet, so he could step across the quagmire.

Bamba saw Boko lying there, but it was not Boko at all, only a spruce branch. And Boko—it was as if he had never been!

Then they started crossing the river. Bamba saw someone's gray locks flapping and green eyes shining in the water.

"Don't go into the water!" Bamba said to Ivan. "You see, Ganka, the old man, is in the water, lying in wait for us! You see, he has stuck out his iron hand!"

Ivan dove into the water and grabbed the gray-haired devil. When he came out of the river, he was holding in his hands a piece of driftwood and a toothy pike that had been hiding under it. Ivan and Bamba ate the pike and went on. Bamba never did see the devil Ganka again.

Then the sworn brothers started to climb a mountain. Bamba was shaking with fear—they were walking in the very place where Kakzamu lay in wait for people. And no sooner did Bamba think about Kakzamu than Kakzamu himself appeared. He opened his red eyes wide and stared at them; he stretched his arms out to them, trying to touch them and turn them to stone.

"Ivan!" shouted Bamba. "Let's run from here, let's run onto the grass—Kakzamu has no power over us there!"

Ivan turned around and struck Kakzamu with his iron stick. All you could see was sparks flying in all directions. Kakzamu's eyes closed. Bamba looked and saw only a gray rock, overgrown with moss; there was no Kakzamu in sight. "He is hiding," thought Bamba. Ivan walked on; Bamba walked behind

him and kept looking back. But there was no Kakzamu there, and that was all there was to it! Ivan's blow had made him vanish.

Then Ivan asked Bamba, "Well, where does your devil Khimu live?"

As he said this, the sworn brothers came out onto a lake, where they saw Khimu already crawling toward them, writhing and breathing fire. Bamba shouted; he wanted to run, but Ivan said to him, "What's the matter, Bamba? Haven't you ever seen fire before?"

Bamba turned around. There was no Khimu—it was as if there never had been.

It was true that grass was burning and fire was crawling along the ground like a snake. It was true that stones were lying in a row, looking like snake scales. But there was no Khimu. Bamba breathed freely again.

Then he saw: there were no devils at all. He and Ivan were standing on their own land—both strong, both brave, both hunters, both bogatyrs, only Ivan was a little older. And all around them everything could be understood: trees grew in the forest, animals lived in the taiga, fish swam in the river, stones lay in the mountains. Bamba thought a while and suddenly he said, "But, then, our tales have disappeared too! Tales about the taiga people, the water people, and the mountain people have all disappeared."

"Never mind," said Ivan, "there will be other tales now! Are you not strong? Are you not brave? Are you not master of your land? Am I not your friend? Won't they make up tales about us?"

From here on, new tales begin. Tales of love and of friendship. Tales of strength and of courage. Tales of skill and of faithfulness. New tales begin about steadfast hearts, strong hands, and unerring eyes.